Surface Paradise

Surface Paradise

Allan Green

iUniverse®

SURFACE PARADISE

iUniverse books may be ordered through booksellers or by contacting:

iUniverse
1663 Liberty Drive
Bloomington, IN 47403
www.iuniverse.com
1-800-Authors (1-800-288-4677)

ISBN: 978-1-4917-6242-4 (sc)
ISBN: 978-1-4917-6243-1 (hc)
ISBN: 978-1-4917-6241-7 (e)

Library of Congress Control Number: 2015905472

Print information available on the last page.

iUniverse rev. date: 04/02/2015

What can ail thee, knight-at-arms,
Alone and palely loitering?
—John Keats, "La Belle Dame Sans Merci"

Praise for Mr. Green's first novel, *Soldier Boy*

Upon receipt of *Soldier Boy,* I sat myself down to read, and I still can't believe what happened. This is absolutely the best story/writing that I have encountered in a very long time. It is a story that draws one in and never lets one go until the very last page, and then the reader doesn't want it to end!

Soldier Boy begins in a small, rural town in Pennsylvania in the 1930s and leads the reader down into the coal mines and details the difficult life a miner would have faced in that time and place.

The main character, Tom, is bright by any standards and vehemently struggles with his domineering father, who subjects him to ridicule and self-esteem lowering verbiage, in order to get his son to give up what his father sees as a pitiful job in a local grocery store and join him down in the depths of the earth. As time goes by, Tom, though he is becoming weary of his father's demeaning attacks, begins to question that he has indeed done the right thing by sticking to his dreams of going to college. And to make matters worse, America has now become involved in events in Europe that eventually draw America into World War II, and Tom, after much agonizing, decides that it is better for him to volunteer to serve in the war and hope it will be over soon. And to further complicate matters, Tom finds that he is attracted to the store owner's daughter and finds that she feels the same attraction to him.

Martha Stevens-David
Magic City Morning Star

1

"Michael darling?"

"Mother, it's open!"

Grace Sykes, in crepe de chine pajamas and a turquoise dressing gown, entered her son's bedroom. Tall, she had the figure of someone much younger. Her gray hair was silvery blue, and she had keen brown eyes that devoured her son. Michael pulled himself up to the head of the bed, baring his chest, and rested his head against the headboard. Stooping to embrace him, his mother kissed one unshaven cheek and then sat on the edge of his bed while he reached for his pack of herbal cigarettes on the night table. He lit one and gratefully exhaled above his head.

"Those cigarettes are so smelly!" Grace exclaimed.

Smiling, Michael felt like a chastised child.

"Will you be going away again?" Grace asked in a worrisome tone. "The past three months, I've worried so much about you, not knowing where you were or if you were being looked after."

"Didn't I write?"

"I don't call the occasional postcard writing."

"I don't wish to write letters, Mother," Michael said.

"Darling, you look so thin," Grace admonished. "When Jud got back, he said you'd been living in a sordid neighborhood."

"Do you call the Latin Quarter in Paris sordid?" Michael asked.

"Where did you stay? It certainly wasn't a proper hotel."

"Monsieur le Prince isn't the George Cinq," Michael conceded.

"You know I've always wanted you to be settled and living nearby, not flitting about the world, and so would your father, if he were still alive. You must build yourself up by living properly and getting sufficient sleep and exercise. When you're feeling up to it, you must speak with Justin about going into the firm, as your father wished."

"I'll need some time to work things out," Michael protested, feeling annoyed as he looked out the sunlit window.

"You should have gone into the firm as soon as you graduated from Harvard, as your father wanted," Grace responded. "Now Justin will be losing patience with you for wasting your time."

Michael frowned, putting out his cigarette in the ashtray.

"I suppose I shouldn't tell you all this?" his mother said.

"About Justin?"

"And your childhood sweetheart."

"Jaine?"

"When Jud got back from Europe, he started seeing Jaine," Grace said. "I thought nothing of it at first, that they were just good friends, but then I saw them necking beneath the copper beech."

Michael looked annoyed but said nothing.

"Don't say that I didn't warn you," Grace said, standing. "Now, darling, you must shave and dress, and please don't tell anyone what I told you."

Michael smiled as if it would be their secret, at least for the time being. He and Jaine had an understanding that one day they would marry, and he hoped she hadn't broken it.

Grace stepped into the bathroom and turned on the hot water to fill the tub. "Don't let it overflow!" she called to her son before departing into the hall.

Michael sat staring at the bright sunlight coming in the open window. As an only child, he'd been smothered by the affection of his parents, and the effects of their indulgence had made him suspicious of all emotion. At boarding school and at Harvard, he'd made a few friends, but most people regarded him as standoffish, if not ironic, for the infinite stores of wisdom he'd derived from Oscar Wilde. Bright, he had no head for math or science, but he read widely in English literature and liked French; a French teacher once told him that he should train to teach that subject, which was the sincerest academic compliment he'd ever received. He was intellectually pretentious, after the fashion of youth, having read Proust, Nietzsche's *Superman*, and the novels of Henry James, none of which would serve to make him a future stockbroker or bond trader.

Michael sprang naked from the bed, dashed into the bathroom, and turned off the water before it overflowed. Bobbing on the steamy surface was the plastic duck his mother had given him as a child. *Has it been here all these years?* Michael asked himself, its inexplicable reappearance striking him as a cloying recrudescence of the maternal instinct. Once immersed, Michael found the water too hot for midsummer; the sweat trickled down his face.

Yes, I've been a disappointment to my father, Michael silently lectured himself. *If I'd been a physician or a lawyer, my destiny would have been certain. But I must become a stockbroker with the prospect of making an intolerable amount of money, although money has its compensations of a material sort.* Each summer they'd sail to Europe on the *Ile de France*, since his mother hated the Cunard line cuisine.

Jack Sykes, Michael's father, was an alert, dapper figure, a good mixer and bridge player who'd emigrated from the North of England with his elder brother as a boy of fifteen. Jack had acquired an American accent that was neither "mouthed" like the speech of the North of England nor clipped like that of the South of England, but it was American; it lacked the twang of the Yankees or a southern drawl, for he spoke "mid-Atlantic."

Jack Sykes was determined and aggressive when he talked about money, wasting no time with preliminaries but getting straight to the point. Needless to say, he always had a specific stock recommendation that came straight from the horse's mouth. For general culture, he had never read a book save for Plutarch's *Lives*, which he'd checked out of the local library at age twenty-one and dutifully read, so that whenever anyone tried to pull the dog on him, he'd rejoin, "Have you read Plutarch's *Lives*?"

With a bath towel about his waist, Michael entered the bedroom, stepped to the window, and kneeled down before it. Beyond the boxwood hedge, Jaine Price was cutting long-stemmed roses of various hues and placing them in a wicker basket.

"Jaine, how 'bout a game of tennis?" Michael called.

"Good morning, sleepyhead!"

"Can you be ready by nine o'clock? It's good to see you!"

"It's good to see you too, Michael!" Jaine said, turning, a smile on her lips.

* * *

Michael's mother was already having breakfast.

"I'll be playing tennis with Jaine after breakfast," Michael said as he sat down opposite her.

On her putting down the *New York Times*, it was clear that Mrs. Sykes wore a smartly tailored, beige pantsuit, and she looked at her son with eyebrows raised. Michael was determined that he would not mention the plastic duck.

Michael loped down the grassy slope to the tennis court, concealed from Long Island Sound by weeping willows whose branches lapped the water. He wore tennis shorts and was carrying his racquet. He sat on the wooden seat encircling the copper beech and gazed back at both houses: his father's redbrick Tudor with its steep, sloping slate roof, brick chimneys, and leaded light windows, and the Prices' Norman chateau next door. Michael's father had bought the house in '31, two years before Michael was born, the previous owner having declared bankruptcy and blown his brains out at the bottom of the Great Depression.

"Michael!" Jaine called, breaking in on his reverie as she bounced down the grassy slope wearing a white tennis outfit and flat-soled shoes. Springing to his feet, Michael clasped her hands and briefly kissed her lips. "Why didn't you write?" Jaine immediately admonished him, sounding like his mother.

"I did."

"Do you call a postcard of the Sacré-Coeur writing, when you'd been away since May?"

"Aren't we going to play tennis?"

"First I must have an answer to my question."

"I didn't go to Europe to write letters! Let's play our game?"

"Okay, I'll let you off this time," Jaine said, smiling, the blue eyes of her china-doll face fixed on him. Her skin was almost as white as porcelain, because she carefully avoided the sun. Her lips were pouty and full, her nose retroussé, and her long blonde hair held tightly in a bun at the back of her head.

As they sat on a bench beneath the copper beech, Michael patted her arm and teased her. He was thinking of a way of asking her about Jud, or was he merely being tactful? At twenty-four, the same age as Michael, Jaine had left the slimness of girlhood behind, and Michael had noticed the fullness of her breasts and her heavy movements when she'd run down the lawn.

"What were you doing in Paris anyway? Chasing French girls?"

"Is that what Jud said?"

"He didn't tell me anything."

"Did he tell you that I went to Spain?"

"Didn't you feel lonely?"

"No, I felt exhilarated."

"Do you like being by yourself?"

"Yes, but I didn't realize how much I'd miss you."

"That's very cool, I must say!" Jaine exclaimed. "But I suppose I had it coming? After all, I've always been sentimental about you. Do you realize that you're the first boy I ever kissed?"

"A seventeen-year-old boy isn't sentimental."

"I didn't say you were, because you've no sentiment," Jaine said, squeezing his nearby knee. "Michael, you do have bony knees! Don't you remember our first kiss?"

"What's this I hear about you and Jud?" Michael asked, ignoring her question.

"How's your asthma?" Jaine responded with calculated inconsequence.

"What do you see in Jud?"

"Michael, you do make my blood boil!"

Michael stood up, repeating his question, "What do you see in Jud, anyway?"

Jaine stood and kicked him in the shin.

"That hurt!" Michael said, clasping his leg and hopping about on the other.

"Actually, Michael, Jud means nothing to me, but you're being so selfish!"

"Don't you want me to be jealous?"

"I don't expect your flattery, for heaven knows I've had precious little of that!" Jaine exclaimed, laughing. "But I've always felt comfortable with you; perhaps that's what went wrong. Do you think we've known each other too long?"

"Jaine, I love you."

"That doesn't sound like flattery!"

"It isn't meant to."

"Oh, Michael!" Jaine cried as he put his arms about her and kissed her.

"I want to make you happy," Michael said, seeing the tears in her eyes.

"I want us both to be very happy," Jaine insisted. "Daddy wants to talk with you."

"Okay, but you must give me a chance."

"Michael, you must be practical so that we can be happy," Jaine insisted.

"Is your father at home now?"

"No, but he'll be here tonight. I spoke with him this morning, and he said he'll see you tomorrow at breakfast."

"Okay, tell him that's fine. Now what about our game?"

"Michael?"

"Yes?"

"Jud means nothing to me."

"Did he get his job at the State Department?"

"Not yet, but he's hoping for Austria."

Justin Price's chateau had been brought over from France as ship's ballast by the previous owner, a rich brewer of the Gilded Age. The following morning at eight thirty, Justin greeted Michael Sykes with a firm handshake under the portico. Gruff and in good spirits, Justin was a fleshy-faced, corpulent man who bore a striking resemblance to J. P. Morgan. He led Michael down a deeply carpeted hall to the oak-paneled dining room, where preparations had been made for a hearty breakfast, which was laid out on the long mahogany sideboard.

"You must find life here rather dull after gay Paree?" Justin said in his deep, resonant voice and with the disconcerting stare of a self-made man as they sat down with Michael on his left.

"I don't feel that I'm back as yet," Michael said. "Last night I got the late train from New York, arriving here at two o'clock this morning."

"I understand from Jaine that you've decided to do some serious work," Justin said, suspiciously eyeing his guest as the steward heaped his plate with scrambled eggs and bacon.

"Admittedly, I haven't made the best use of my time in recent years," Michael said, taken aback by Justin's directness.

"I like a man with ambition, just as I hate indecision," Justin said, thrusting a crisp of bacon into his mouth.

"I know that my father admired you for your ambition," Michael responded, wishing to say something flattering.

"Your father and I were excellent partners," Justin said with a broad smile. "We were both self-made men, you see, men who knew their own interest. I trust you'll follow in your father's footsteps?"

"I'm grateful to you for the confidence you've shown in me," Michael said, conscious of the importance of being acquiescent.

"You will begin with fixed-income securities," Justin announced, riveting his dark, magnetic eyes upon the young man.

"Fixed-income securities?"

"Bonds. Come to the office on Monday, and I'll give you some pointers and show you some things that'll change your life."

"I'm grateful for the opportunity."

"I started out in Columbus, Ohio, working in a shoe factory, but I was determined to rise. When I got to New York, I worked at anything, always had an iron in the fire. I studied finance nights at New York University and made my first million before I was thirty, but lost it in the Crash of Twenty-Nine. Two years later I was back on my feet and bought this place the same year your father bought his next door."

"Again, I'm very grateful to have the opportunity," Michael said at the end of the hour.

"Lemme show you to the door," Justin pulled himself to his feet and lumbering down the carpeted passage to the front portico, where he subjected Michael to his viselike grip, saying, "I'll see you at the office on Monday morning then?"

"Yes, on Monday, sir," Michael said, turning into the bright sunlight.

4

That afternoon Michael drove Jaine in his mother's canary Cadillac Coupe de Ville convertible with leopard-skin seats to McGrath's Beach, a short stretch of the North Shore of Long Island, where rich families have banded together for many years behind an enclosure of chain-link fence. Jaine wore a white sundress over her bathing suit, and Michael was conscious of the glow that radiated from her face. When she turned and smiled at him, there was a flash of light in her warm brown eyes.

She slipped close beside him and placed her hand on his leg, squeezing it as she said, "You kept me waiting."

"Did I?" Michael asked, revving the engine.

As he drove, the hot summer fields rolled away, giving the pair a sense of exhilaration so that they began to feel a part of each other, as if they were making love for the first time. Thrusting her arm about Michael's waist, Jaine leaned her head on his shoulder. "Perfect. Don't you think life is perfect?" she asked him, a smile on her lips. She took off her kerchief about her head so that her golden hair trailed behind her, and on her lips appeared a conscious smile of love.

"Michael!" Jaine suddenly cried, alarmed at the speed they were going. "Are you crazy?"

He eased back, and the landscape slowed. He turned and noticed the fear in her eyes.

"Promise me you won't do that again!" she exclaimed. "Do you want to get us both killed or for you to get a ticket?"

"Doesn't your father have the pull to fix tickets?" Michael asked.

Jaine did not reply, but instead brooded on Michael's unattractive side.

When they reached the gate, John McGrath, whose family had been potato farmers for three generations, tipped his cap, and Michael and Jaine proceeded to a blind of pine trees, where Michael drew up beneath the trees. They walked the short distance onto the beach, leaving the sunbathers and splashing children at a distance along the shore. Michael spread out the blanket and pulled off his polo shirt, and Jaine unzipped her sundress, revealing a one-piece bathing suit.

"Pretty neat!" Michael exclaimed, smiling at her.

"Are you really happy to work for my dad?" Jaine asked as she sat down on the blanket beside him.

"I'll give it a try."

"For my sake?"

"Yeah."

"Then you'll make us both miserable!"

"Why do you say that?"

"It must be what you want."

"Jaine, lemme explain."

"When I saw you yesterday, I sensed that you weren't the same person who'd sailed to Europe with Jud in May. You'd changed for the worse."

"Look, Jaine, I'm not going to lie to you, so why should I tell you that I'm going to like it? I won't find selling bonds particularly noble, worthwhile, or even desirable. All I told your father was that I'd give it a try. Maybe I'll like it. Who knows? After all, I have my father behind me, who practiced the fine art of fleecing people for thirty years."

"How can you say such a thing?"

"Do you prefer me to lie? I said I'll give it a try, so why can't I at least be honest with you? If I can't, I'll soon find the walls closing about me."

"You are a very different person," Jaine insisted. "There are times when I find you callous and egotistical, not the person I knew."

"You want everything to fit perfectly, but it can't. Life's not like that. It's full of uncertainties, failures, and plans that must be scrapped. Nothing's predestined, nor would I wish it to be. Don't you see that?"

"I suppose you're afraid of losing your freedom. That's what your fine words are all about. You've never taken life seriously."

"It's because I take it seriously that I've wish to experience it," Michael protested. "Certainly I don't want anything to be predetermined, least of all about us." Pausing, he stared into the sky, which had been darkened by a cloud. "It would mean a great deal to me if you felt as I do. Then all our feelings would be realized."

"But, Michael, I can't help feeling fearful," Jaine said.

"But when we're married, our path will be the same," Michael insisted, lying back in the sand and covering his eyes with his right hand.

"Do you want to have a lot of children?" Jaine asked, staring down into his eyes.

"Yes, I'd like a big family."

"Won't children affect your sense of freedom?"

"No."

Placing her head on Michael's chest, Jaine began to cry, for to her it seemed that a wedge had been driven between them. They'd opened their hearts, because from childhood their hearts had been one, but now she felt that they were two different people.

Late in the afternoon they folded their blanket under a darkening sky. Michael put the top up on the Cadillac, for the pine trees were swaying as the first gusts of a thunderstorm approached. On the drive back, they hardly spoke a word, and when Michael stopped beneath the portico of the Prices' French provincial house, Jaine jumped out without saying good-bye and dashed indoors. The rain was beating against the windows and whipping the treetops.

For a moment Michael listened to the wail of the wind in the trees, telling himself that he was a bastard for letting his ego get in the way of his love for Jaine.

He didn't wish to go indoors. So when he'd parked his mother's Cadillac in the garage, he waited for the rain to cease. As soon as he could, he walked down the grassy slope to the tennis court, beyond which was a screen of weeping willows along the shore by a narrow strip of beach. The Sound was being lashed by a thunderstorm out of the northeast; it was early for the season.

Michael met Tony Palmieri at the Venezuelan Line at the foot of Fourteenth Street in Brooklyn. A heavyset figure with iron-gray hair, Tony knew the simple pleasures of life. Their shoes rang on the cobblestones as they walked to a diner with a clock on the outside wall, which said it was ten to five. They ordered burgers and coffee from the red-haired waitress but didn't have to wait long for service because there were few customers at that hour. Both men wore chinos, and they took off their windbreakers because it was heated in the place, even though it was the end of September.

"Watcha bin doin', Tony?" Michael asked in a tone of affection.

"Bin hangin' out at my brother's house in Hoboken," Tony said. "Like I tol' ya, I'm shippin' out dis Friday on de *Excalibur* for Sout' 'merica."

"Tony, can I come along?"

"You axed me dat twice already. Watcha wanna go back for?"

"How 'bout I need a job?"

"Dare ain't no job," Tony insisted. "Besides, dis life ain't fer you, Mike. Make somethin' of yerself fer crissake. Become a lawyer, an' rob people."

"I dunno."

"Whatcha wanna be driftin' 'bout wid nothin' ta show fer it?" Tony asked. "All I wan' is a rundown farm over in Pennsy, which I saw in a picture. Can't ya see me keepin' pigs an' chickens an' listenin' ta da silence? When ya git worn out in dis business dey trow ya out 'cause yer a has-been, but I'll 'ave diz place ta go."

"What about the *Excalibur*?" Michael persisted.

"She sails at five o'clock on Friday mornin'."

"Do you ever do a friend a favor?"

"Neber."

"I gotta get on a ship."

"What's wid you, Mike?"

"I gotta find a ship."

"Okay, be dare when she sails, an' I see what I can do."

An hour later Michael walked into a street of brownstones in Lower Manhattan. The street was deserted, which wasn't unusual, for even at the busiest hours of the day no one ventured there. Some of the buildings were boarded up; some had broken windows with a look of desolation and neglect.

He had come upon this street from the light-pulsing artery of Broadway, searching for a particular window. Having found it, he climbed the steps, entered the hallway, and began to climb the stairs in near darkness. He stopped before the door of the rear apartment and rapped sharply, persistently on it. A potbellied man with a fringe of white hair encircling his pate peered at him out of frightened eyes, as he tightened the drawstring of his dressing gown about his ample girth.

"Ambrose, where's Antoinette?"

"Look here!"

"Ambrose, who is it?" came the woman's voice from within.

Michael quickly jammed his foot in the door and, pushing the bald man aside, entered the artist's studio. The pictures adorning the walls were all of the same woman, a woman of dark, sultry beauty, dressed as if she'd lived in Andalusian Spain or in Italy at the time of the Borgias.

"Get out!" Michael ordered Ambrose, having finished his rapid survey of the room.

Ambrose left, and Michael stepped past the bedroom door, which had been left ajar, where the dark-haired woman in a chartreuse dressing gown was seated before a vanity.

"Michael!" she exclaimed, jumping up, her face revealed harshly by the naked light bulb hanging from a cord above the double bed. An autumn haze smoked in her eyes, which were tender and softly luminous, a quality they shared with the happy days of her past. Her dressing gown was loosely drawn, revealing her magnificent breasts, a temptation to the eyes. She was a lovely vision of a mature Venus as she encircled Michaels's neck and pressed a burning kiss on his lips. He opened his eyes to the blue veins of her eyelids, which she opened to reveal the flame that glowed within.

"I'm still your Antoinette, ain't I, Michael, darling?" she asked, her hands passing inside his windbreaker.

"When I give you money, I don't want you livin' with somebody," Michael protested as he pushed her away.

"How was I to know you'd be comin' back when you don't even bother to write?" Antoinette challenged him.

"But I sent you money for rent and for food."

"Mike, it's not what you think about Ambrose and me. He sleeps in the daybed in the studio and doesn't bother me."

"Doesn't he look at you all day in the buff?" Michael asked.

"Ambrose is an artist. I could be that chair as far as he's concerned."

"But he isn't blind!"

"I'm not going to argue with you on the point, darling," Antoinette insisted, her tone softening as she placed her hands on his ears, and again they kissed. Then she raised the dressing gown over her shoulders and let it fall to the floor, the light from the window shining on her full figure. She helped him to undress and lifted the bedclothes.

"How beautiful you are," Michael said in a breath.

"Don't be silly!" Antoinette said, smiling. "Sometimes I wonder if you know anything about me."

"I'm happy to be with you. Isn't that enough?"

"You're a mystery to me, which I find hard to explain. You're educated, but you don't do anything with it."

"Don't worry about that," Michael protested, kissing her breasts, then looking into her eyes. "You trust me, don't you?"

"Trust yourself first," Antoinette responded, a warm light glowing in her eyes.

* * *

Michael remained in bed and watched her dress, putting on a bright-red dress with silver sequins. Then she sat at the vanity and began applying her lipstick, every stroke the work of an artist.

"Don't you want to get something to eat, Mike?" Antoinette asked.

"Where?"

"What about that Italian place, just on the corner of Broadway?"

"Sure. Okay."

Outside was the chill of autumn twilight. They walked a few blocks to the restaurant and went downstairs. Even though there were few customers, they sat at a table way at the back.

"What are you going to order, Mike?"

"I dunno, maybe a burger."

"Doan' be silly. This is an Italian restaurant."

"You order for both of us then."

"What do you like?"

"Whatever you like."

The waiter came over, a tomato-stained apron about his paunch, and produced a pad, his stubby pencil poised to take their order.

"Mike, what do you like?" Antoinette again asked.

"I'll have the French toast and a cup of lemon tea," he told the waiter.

"No," Antoinette informed the waiter, smiling.

"When you've made up your minds, lemme know," the waiter said, going off.

"You must not be very hungry?" Antoinette asked.

"How can you live with Ambrose?"

"You don't understand."

"Has he sold any paintings of you?"

"Lots."

"Does he give you half?"

"You must be jokin'!"

"He should pay for the privilege of leering at you."

"Mike, you can't turn up after all these months and expect everything to be the same," Antoinette insisted, her voice hardening. "Why are you going to South America?"

"Are you going to marry Ambrose?"

"We haven't set a date."

"You've still got your sense of humor," Michael conceded, smiling.

Antoinette remembered taking Michael home to Brooklyn, where her parents owned a deli, living above it. She'd expected him to be critical or to act as if he were slumming—that had been the worst part of her fear; but he'd helped Mama in the kitchen and questioned Papa about Naples, telling him he'd been there. Then, after the last voyage about a year ago, he'd come to Woolworth's, where she'd been selling cosmetics, and he'd taken her out to an expensive restaurant. He'd told her that he loved her and had missed her very much, but he'd gone away, and she hadn't seen him for months.

He remained an enigma to her. Maybe she'd get to know him. Maybe she'd never get to know him better than she did now. Or maybe he wasn't serious when he said that he loved her and wanted to marry her.

"When are we going to order?" Antoinette reminded him.

"I haven't seen the menu."

"If you did, what would you order?"

"Eggs and bacon."

"That's why you haven't seen the menu."

"Okay, you order."

"I'm having minestrone and lasagna, the way my mother cooks it," Antoinette reminded him.

"Yeah, nobody beats your mother's cooking!"

"I really guess I should explain about Ambrose," Antoinette remarked matter-of-factly when the meal was over and they were sipping their cappuccinos. "He doesn't mean anything to me, but I needed the money, and he offered me a job."

"What happened to the money I sent you to take a secretarial course?" Michael demanded.

"I gave it to my kid brother, Tony. Do you remember him?"

"It doesn't matter."

"What doesn't matter?"

"Nothin'."

"I gave it to him so he didn't have to work full time, and he'll pay me back."

"It doesn't matter; forget it."

Antoinette began rummaging in her handbag, as women do when they're agitated. When she looked up again, she saw the smile on his face, which looked beautiful; it was a radiant smile of understanding, so it didn't matter.

"Do you promise you won't leave me again?" Antoinette asked.

"I never left you before," Michael replied.

When they left the restaurant, they walked to Washington Square, where Michael bought a bag of peanuts. They sat on a bench and ate the peanuts, feeding some to the pigeons.

"Oh, Michael, I feel so happy," Antoinette announced, putting her arms about him as they kissed.

"I want you to come and live with me in Paris."

"Paris?"

"Yes."

"When?"

"Now! We'll speak French and travel about on the Continent!"

"What about money?"

"Don't worry about money."

"Michael, you're very romantic!" Antoinette exclaimed, squeezing him.

* * *

At four thirty on Friday morning, Michael found Tony Palmieri at the diner in Brooklyn. In the garish light, Tony looked tired, older than his years, slumped in a booth, his face dull.

"What's the matter, Tony?"

"Dings hab been better."

"Did you ever do a friend a favor?"

"No, neber."

"I gotta find a ship."

"Fer crissake, ya've bin home a week and awready ya wanns ship out. Whatsit wid ya?"

"When's the *Excalibur* sailing?"

"Dis mornin' at five o'clock. Whatcha bin doin' wid yerself?"

"Hanging 'round."

"Wid dat Brooklyn dame ya tol' me 'bout once't?"

Michael hunched over, pressing the heels of his hands into his eye sockets.

"Okay, Mike, ya've got da job. Dat make ya happy?"

"Thanks, Tony," Michael said, with a hapless grin.

"Ya doan' know whatcha want, and here I am shovin' sixty an' all I wan' is ta spend the rest of my days tillin' da soil and keepin' pigs and chickens and maybe a few cows. Sumtimes I feel I'm goin' crazy just dinkin' 'bout dat farm!"

They walked to the pier, where the masts of the vessel rose before them. Soon the hot South American sun would blister their faces. They walked side by side, the strides of the younger man slowing down to accommodate the pace of the older. A few lights on the vessel wore misty halos. Far off they heard the wail of a siren.

"Mike, dis has been my life," Tony confessed sadly. "I'm always shovin' off, and when I first seed you, I said to myself, dis kid wid white hands neber worked a day in his life. So what I'm tryin' ta say, Mike, is dat you should find somethin' better."

Again came the distant wail of the siren as they climbed the gangway.

6

"How ya doin', Mike—come on in!" Judson Jones greeted Michael as he opened the door of his house.

"I have a date for a game of tennis with Jaine," Michael said.

"Jaine tol' me she'll be down in a moment," Judson replied as he pumped Michael's arm in an excess of energy. His black eyes radiated beneath bushy brows as the longtime college friends slumped in chairs in the living room.

"Ya comin' over for lunch?" Judson asked.

"Am I invited?"

"Come off it, Mike!" Judson exclaimed, laughing. "Ever since you lost your mother, you've been alone too much."

"I don't like dressing for dinner."

"Who said anything 'bout dressin' for dinner?"

"Okay, I'll come."

"Look, Mike, can I talk to you like a brother for a moment?"

"Sure, shoot."

"Las' year, ever since you came into Sykes, Price, and Company, ya've acted as if nothin' mattered to ya, like ya'd lost yer illusions."

"Look, Jud, I promised my mother I'd go into the business, but—"

"So you've up and joined the Merchant Marines?" Jud interjected with a wry smile.

"That was a steady job, wasn't it?" Michael said, meeting his smile.

"Look, lemme lay it ta ya: has the way ya've been feelin' anything ta do with Jaine and I gettin' hitched las' year?" Judson asked, his black eyes fixed on his friend.

"Believe me, no," Michael insisted, hunching over.

"Honest injun?"

"Jud, would I have been best man at your wedding if I'd felt like that?"

"Thanks, Mike, I'll remember that," Judson replied. "But listen, if you're not happy with the firm, is it just because you've got wanderlust in your soul? If so, why don't you do what I was plannin' ta do before I came into the business?"

"Join the State Department, you mean, and be sent to some godforsaken hole?"

"Vienna isn't a godforsaken hole."

"Actually, Jud, since my mother died, I've given the idea some thought, but I decided I'd stay at home and eat Roquefort cheese."

"Hah hah! That's a good one, Mike!"

"Ya know, I always felt like your brother, and when you came into the firm, I had the highest hopes that we'd be a perfect fit."

"But it didn't work out that way, did it?"

"Whose fault was that?"

"I don't say it was anybody's fault, Mike. I'm merely stating a fact."

"Ya know, sometimes I feel guilty about havin' come between you and Jaine."

"Jud, that's not the case at all, lemme—"

"All's fair in love and war, right?"

"Yeah, somethin' like that."

"Mike, are you stayin' for lunch?" Jaine asked, appearing in her pleated tennis dress and holding her racquet, her blonde hair tied back in a ponytail.

"I've already asked him," Judson said.

"I thought I'd made my excuse, but now I see that it's my duty to stay," Michael conceded as he embraced Jaine, kissing her on the cheek.

* * *

Michael and Jaine walked side by side down the grassy slope to the tennis court screened by a line of weeping willows, obscuring the view of the Sound sparkling in the bright September sunlight. Pausing, they looked back at the redbrick English Tudor where Michael now lived alone. The housekeeper, Mrs. Tucker, cooked his meals and cleaned, but she didn't live there, instead residing in the nearby village.

Michael controlled the first set, allowing Jaine but two games. She blamed her defeat on not having played in some time, but she knew that she would despise him if he threw the set. Afterward they sat on the wooden bench beneath the copper beech near the court.

"What the devil are you running away from, Mike?" Jaine suddenly asked in the spirit of old comradeship.

"Jud was just on to me. He thinks I should join the French Foreign Legion," Michael replied, smiling.

"The French Foreign Legion?" Jaine asked, her eyes opening wide.

"The State Department, to be sent to Timbuktu!" Michael exclaimed, laughing.

They walked up the lawn and entered the house through the French doors, where a portrait of Grace Sykes greeted them, gazing down from above the marble fireplace. She was smartly dressed in a tailored suit, painted standing before her canary Cadillac Coupe de Ville, with luggage stowed in the trunk. She was about to sail to Europe on the *Ile de France.*

"What are you reading now?" Jaine asked, seeing the books scattered on the coffee table.

"Mainly Proust."

"I tried him—once."

"He takes time," Michael explained. "Shall I change for lunch?"

"Give me a cigarette."

"Over there," Michael said, nodding at the mantelpiece.

"Not one of your herbal ones?"

"No," Michael said, laughing as he dashed upstairs.

He pulled his T-shirt over his head and was stepping out of his shorts when he heard Jaine's voice coming from the adjacent bathroom, "Whose plastic duck is this?"

"When I was a kid, my mother gave it to me," he said, quickly pulling on his shorts again as Jaine entered his bedroom.

"Ain't I a bold hussy?" Jaine asked, a mischievous smile on her lips. "Who would think we'd been friends since childhood? Heck knows, we're like brother and sister. Besides, you've got to remember that life isn't like a novel."

"Usually novels are better."

"Mike, if life doesn't live up to your expectations, whose fault is that?"

"I find that there are all kinds of people in the world, and most of them don't sell bonds."

"So that's it? Do you mean to run away again, because you feel a failure?"

"Is that what Jud thinks?"

"Admit it; your pride's hurt."

"I confess that I really don't want to sell bonds."

"Does that mean you must join the merchant navy? I see that you're as confused as ever."

"At least you see through me," Michael replied, a hint of mockery in his voice. "My refusal to accept responsibility is a sure sign of my immaturity. That's what I should have told Jud, but I didn't, for reasons I can't explain or concede, even to myself, for I'm not enough of a bastard. The fact is that I've taken a job with the State Department. They're not sending me to Austria, but Australia."

"Australia!"

"Yeah, to Terra Australia Incognita," Michael confessed. "When I told the bloke at the State Department—I've gotta use the Aussie lingo, you see—that I wanted to be posted to Austria 'cause I like to ski, he replied, 'How 'bout Australia?' 'Why Australia?' I asked. ''Cause we've got an opening there—an' it begins with an A, just like Austria.'"

"So you can't plan on winter sports. That's for sure!" Jaine exclaimed, laughing in spite of herself. "But, Mike, how could you?"

"I've allowed myself to vegetate for long enough."

Jaine stood before him, her heavenly blue eyes telling him that she wasn't happy. "Jud and I are trying to have a baby."

"I'm sorry."

"You're not sorry! Jud won't see a doctor. So we have no basis for our marriage."

"I'm sorry."

"You're not sorry!"

"I said I'm sorry!"

"Don't say you're sorry, because I hate him!"

"You really don't know what you're saying."

"Why shouldn't I hate him if my marriage is a hoax? There's nothing more that can be said."

"I'm sorry."

"Stop staying that. Remember you're going to Australia. Why can't I come with you?" As he put his arms about her, she began sobbing. "I guess we're both failures," she conceded.

"Jud got the job because you married him," Michael insisted.

"An' you lost yours because you're so much better than other people!" Jaine fired back.

"You're right when you say that I have no real plans."

"Why shouldn't I hate Jud?" Jaine asked, her blue eyes fixed on his with a smile. "My love for him was no more than my desire to get even with you. May I have a shower?" She began to undress, her breasts full, her body bright in the sunlight that streamed through the open window. Pushing him back on the bed, she lay down above him, her breasts greeting his eyes. In the fierceness of their emotion, they journeyed separately through darkness, despite the brightness of the sunlight that poured upon them.

It had come to this: the empty house—the empty world—lay all about them, unfathomable, continually breaking away and spinning off into the blackness of space. The moment of surrender had been the cry of seagulls wheeling above the roof, as slowly the world returned with the rustling of leaves outside in the September breeze.

"Hey, are you two up there?" Jud's voice rang out.

"Jud," Jaine whispered, biting Michael's ear. "Talk to him while I'm taking a shower."

A moment later Jaine was gone, and Michael heard Judson's footsteps outside.

"Come in!" Michael called, quickly pulling up his tennis shorts.

It was late September—spring Down Under—when Michael reached Sydney, Australia, and began working in the visa section of the American Legation on Elizabeth Street with red-faced Aussies who were convinced that their future lay in the Great Republic. He'd rented a bungalow at Mosman on the North Shore, taken the ferry across Sydney Harbor past the Coat Hanger, as the Aussies fondly call their bridge, and docked at the Circular Quay. Then he'd taken the Underground to Town Hall Station, close to the Legation. Everywhere the yellow wattles were in bloom, and centered in the grass plot before his bungalow with its red-tiled roof and deep verandah grew an improbable bottlebrush tree with its red bottlebrushes stuck on the tips of its branches.

Australia reminded Michael of Greece, which he'd visited as a child with his parents, for it had the blue sky, eternal sunshine, and dry landscape of a Mediterranean country. As soon as he'd stepped off the long Pan Am flight from LA, he'd fallen in love with Australia, feeling that he was at the end of the world, and if he didn't watch out, he might fall into the ether. So rather than feeling lonely, Michael had done what is sacred to the Aussies on the weekends: going to the Northern beaches—Manly, Curl Curl, and Dee Why—to watch the sheilas and drink cold tinnies. Once he'd taken the train out to Katoomba and gone bushwalking in the Blue Mountains from the Jenolan Caves Guest House, where he'd eaten English scones with blackberry jam and Devonshire clotted cream with his tea.

Sydney, with its Victorian public buildings, was "London in the sunshine," as some wag once put it, but the necklace of coastal cities encircled the forbidding Outback, the Back-of-the-Beyond, the Never-Never, where the Aborigines had done walkabouts for twenty centuries across the sacred landscape from soak hole to soak hole, while the Aussies hummed along on the nine-to-five job, with the nagging wife, the kids, and the feeling that the walls were closing in.

So the only freedom Michael had was dreaming that he'd cast off the trammels of civilization, gone bush, or maybe even gone combo with a lubra to live in a humpy in the Outback. Talk about venting one's spleen. He'd resented the dull routine of modern civilization—or was it only his sense of boredom?

Michael had been clueless those first days Down Under, not understanding Strine, the incomprehensible Australian language. He'd spent hours in the reading room of the Mitchell Library, reading that the Aussies were bound each-to-each by "mateyness," which couldn't definitely be defined, at least by foreigners—or even Aussies, for that matter. It meant many things, like the Aussies' perfect indifference to rules and regulations, or enforced discipline. During the First World War, the Aussies didn't need discipline to prove their worth as fighting men. The Limeys on the parade ground were a sight to behold, but who did you side with when the chips were down?

At the American Legation, Michael worked beside plain-spoken Ralph Murchison, an Aussie who'd been hired to translate Strine to Yankees—that was the joke, anyway. One hot November Sunday, Ralph invited his Yankee mate to meet his sister, Gloria. He had never mentioned that he had a sister, so the invite had caused Michael to wonder if he should put him off easily. What did it really matter, anyway?

Gloria's flat was a third-floor walk-up in a terrace house in Paddington, where tea had been a conglomeration of fish paste spread on Ryvita and Vegemite spread on cream crackers, which had the collective effect of giving Michael a queasy stomach. There was a certain hauteur about Gloria, suggestive of pride. She wasn't matey and didn't riddle her speech with Aussie slang, so Michael concluded that it was an odd family that could produce a brother and sister who were so different.

But even Ralph's sense of mateyness didn't go too far, for Michael always felt that if he left Australia and returned a year later, Ralph would say, "Where ya bin, mate?" as if the interval hadn't existed. It wasn't Ralph's fault, really; it was just the casual way of the Aussies.

Gloria wasn't casual, and she wouldn't miss you if you went away. That day at tea she fixed her big, inquiring brown eyes on Michael as if she would question him on a variety of topics. He had learned from Ralph that she was a fashion editor for *Australian Woman*, and she looked a fashion plate herself, taken from one of her magazines. Chic as Gloria was and as knowledgeable of the feminine arts of beauty, she was too conscious of the effect she produced. With her wide-ranging mind, she could speak knowledgeably of social, political, and cultural issues, but she began by challenging him on a lighter tone.

"Has my brother indoctrinated you with all the prejudices of the Australian male?" Gloria asked, sitting at the table across from Michael, before the wrought-iron balcony.

"I'm not aware of that," he replied untruthfully as he spread Vegemite on a cream crack. "Oops!" The cream cracker had broken in two, dropping on his lap, so that he had jumped up.

"Here, let me sponge it!" Gloria insisted, dabbing at the fly of his pants with the dishcloth. With the damage rectified, Gloria sat down again, fixing her eyes on him, while he was busy cementing Vegemite to another cream cracker.

"Australian men despise women and can't get away from them fast enough," Gloria announced. "Or haven't you had time to notice?"

"I don't think of Australia as an enlightened country," Michael replied evasively, raising his eyebrows to meet Gloria's gaze. "But weren't you the first to introduce women's suffrage?"

"Yes, and the secret ballot, compulsory education of children, fixed wages, arbitration of labor disputes, old age pensions—you name it."

"What about the White Australia Policy?" Michael asked, conscious that he was putting his foot in his mouth, for Ralph would resent his attitude. "Is that an enlightened policy?"

"Yer bloody right it is!" Ralph exploded like a gored bull. "We can be friends with the Asiatics without wantin' 'em down here!"

"You Yanks don't have such a wonderful record with the Negroes, right?" Gloria challenged, but more temperately than her brother.

"I don't defend our record with the Negroes," Michael replied. "But what has that got to do with the White Australia Policy?"

"Look, mate, we don't want yer WOP gangsters down 'ere, either," Ralph barked, red-faced. "Besides, I find that countries with mixed races doan' get on so well. Look at India with Hindus cuttin' Muslim throats and Muslims cuttin' Hindu throats."

"We live in a British society, where we're very cozy and complacent," Gloria affirmed.

"Well, in the future you'll trade with Asian countries, so you will have to relax your immigration policies," Michael said.

"Both our Liberal and Labour parties are in agreement in opposing immigration reform," Gloria insisted.

"Pig Iron Bob Menzies won't be prime minister forever," Michael said.

"What's wrong with Pig Iron Bob?" Ralph asked, incredulous.

"He's an anachronism, like Churchill in Forty-Five," Michael insisted.

"Menzies won't tolerate opposition; he'll gag the press," Ralph predicted.

"Do you want a prime minister who will tolerate only sycophants?" Michael countered.

"I'm in favor of reform of all kinds," Gloria insisted, fixing her lustrous brown eyes upon Michael. "But not even I have reached the view that we should open the doors to Asian immigration."

"That would betray the coves who fought the Japs," Ralph said, glowering. "Our trade is with Britain, and that's where we get most of our immigrants."

"You didn't have the British fleet to defend you in Forty-One," Michael said, trying to make Ralph see reason. "Australia is a part of Asia, and someday you'll have to come to terms with that. Right now you've got thousands of Asian students studying here; don't you think they might want to stay?"

"As far as I'm concerned, when they've finished their education, they can go back home," Ralph insisted.

"If we are to have immigration reform, it must be legislated," Gloria said in an effort to raise the tone of the conversation. "It must be the will of the Australian people."

"Let's hope it never 'appens!" Ralph interjected. "Did those coves who died defendin' Oz do so of their own free will? An' come to think of it, did the Yanks come into the war of their own free will? Who legislates these things?"

"My brother's afraid he'll wake up one morning and find the country flooding with Asiatics," Gloria said.

"Too right!" Ralph exclaimed. "An' the gov'mint won't let us vote on it!"

"Well, I certainly have no fear of finding a little yellow man hiding beneath my bed!" Gloria exclaimed, laughing.

"Australia has the reputation of being reactionary," Michael observed, throwing caution to the wind. "You backed the Dutch in Indonesia, and now the Dutch are gone, and the Indonesians have got independence with their populous nation on your doorstep, regarding you as its enemy."

"Should we cease to be a British nation?" Gloria asked with a touch of acerbity.

"No, but you must be Australian," Michael rejoined.

"Cultivate our national myth?" Gloria asked, a mocking light in her eyes.

"Yeah, we'll find it in the Bush," Ralph interjected.

"Why does the Australian male wish to escape from civilization?" Gloria asked Michael.

"Because he's bored with it?" Michael said, smiling at her.

The rest of the visit was less contentious, for they all took the tram to Bondi Beach and swam.

* * *

A few weeks later Ralph invited his friend to spend the Christmas "hols" at Surface Paradise in Queensland, where his mother lived. Ralph held out the prospect of lazing in the sun, and as for Gloria, he needn't worry, for she was taking a hiking holiday on the South Island of New Zealand. Michael read quietly in the Mitchell Library before taking the train to Queensland. The day before he left, he finally got a letter from Antoinette, to whom he'd written often during his first lonely weeks Down Under. He'd carried her letter in his pocket for a day or two before reading it on the ferry to Mosman.

New York
December 9, 195—

Dear Mike,

Delighted that you should write me so much about your first impressions of Australia. Why did you go there if you hate it so much?

Nothing much has happened with me, so how could I write and say nothing? I've never loved Ambrose, but now I realize that you must be free to find yourself. So please don't talk to me about love. You say those things only because we're far away and think that we'll never see each other again.

> Really, Mike, how different can two people be? I recognize that now. So good luck to you and wish me good luck too. You sound older. Are you? Or is that just your letter? Here's an Xmas kiss from miles and miles away—three of them.
>
> XXX
> Love,
> Antoinette

Standing by the rail, Michael tore the blue air letter into pieces and watched as a gust of wind caught them in the bright sunlight, the light of reason, voyagers into the unknown.

8

The heat was intense, and the soot from the locomotive pouring through the open carriage windows smudged Michael's white cord suit. During the interminable night, his asthma had flared up, making him sneeze, and his eyes and nose ran continuously. All morning he stared out the carriage window at the monotonous, dry landscape. The gum trees raised their gnarled limbs against the blue sky in imitation of yoga devotees, the trees' long, narrow, pale-green leaves angled against the sun, preserving what little moisture they could get.

Now and then the train would pass across a dry creek bed, its course marked by nondescript brush or clumps of dry spinifex grass. In the Wet, the rains would come again after fire caused by lightning had scorched the seed cast on the cracked earth, awaiting the rejuvenation of spring. The Australian landscape was alien to everything that Michael had known; he remembered the spring of misty Long Island, when great cumulus clouds like Spanish galleons brought the fresh gusts of rain to the bosom of Long Island Sound.

Early in the afternoon, the train paused for a few minutes at Murwillumba, close to the border of Queensland. Michael, along with most of the other passengers, descended to the snack bar, where they ate meat pies and drank orange squash. As he walked back and forth beside the train, eating a blood-red orange, Michael's hair was the same color and looked like straw, his angular body rangy and bony. His pale-brown eyes were watery, and he looked upon the world as if he were myopic. When he'd finished his orange, he lit an herbal cigarette and climbed aboard the train to stand between the carriages, watching the unpainted wooden buildings that marked the outskirts of town as the train slipped past into the heat and red dust.

Late that afternoon, the train reached Southport, where taxis stood before the station opposite a park, and palm trees raised their lacy umbrellas. Ralph was nowhere to be seen. Michael set down his suitcase, which he tapped rhythmically with his toe, thinking that he should have spent the Christmas vacation at the Mitchell Library in Sydney. He lit another herbal cigarette, drawing in the smoke gratefully before crossing the street to the park and sitting on a bench. In the middle was a pond with a bronze dolphin, corroded green, a jet of water shooting from its mouth into the green, stagnant pool. On the farther side of the park was the main shopping street, with wooden buildings canopied to protect pedestrians from the sun as much as the rain, for when the Wet came, they were prepared, the gutters sufficiently deep to receive Noah's flood.

Closing his eyes, Michael recalled seeing the empty house beneath the overarching elms on the North Shore of Long Island. The house was empty now because his mother had been dead for two years, a victim of black ice, her car suddenly skidding off the road into the creek and breaking through the ice into the water, in which she drowned. Mrs. Tucker still supervised everything, making sure the lawn was cut and the oil tank filled in preparation for winter. His mother's portrait still looked down from the marble mantelpiece in the living room in the blank grayness of winter or in the sunlight glinting on the Sound. On the mantelpiece also was a photograph of him as a child in knickerbockers, seated between his parents in the hotel garden in Lausanne near Lake Geneva.

Returning to the train station, Michael asked about a bus to Surface Paradise; but quickly changing his mind, he toted his suitcase across the park to the canopied buildings that marked Main Street.

Pausing before a liquor store, he noted the cutout cardboard liquor bottles in the window, for evidently the Queensland Government had little faith in its citizens, believing they'd smash the windows to get at the booze.

At the next corner, Michael stepped off the deep gutter and approached a Holden pickup with "Pedrick's Garage, Surface Paradise" painted on the door and a grizzle-faced young man peering out.

"Can you give me a lift to Surface Paradise? I'll pay you."

"Git in, but I doan' want yer lolly. I'm goin' there anyway."

Michael opened the door, thrust his suitcase into the black cavity behind the seat, and hopped in. The pickup lurched forward, the engine sputtering and jolting, sending a pink plastic female nude in erotic gyrations about the dashboard.

"Are ya a Pom?"

"No, I'm an American."

"A Yank?" the driver asked, giving him a dubious look.

"Yeah, my name's Michael Sykes, and I work for the American Legation in Sydney. I've come here to visit a friend."

"So where's he now?"

"I dunno."

"I'm John Pedrick," the driver announced, squirting tobacco juice into the evening. "Ya sure you ain't a Pom? 'Cause ya doan' talk like a Yank."

"Is this your place, Pedrick's Garage?" Michael asked, seeing the sand-colored building with two pumps out front.

"I'll drop ya off at Paradise Avenue."

"Thanks!"

A few minutes later, Michael was toting his suitcase along Paradise Avenue, past a finger in an advertisement that pointed to a beer garden where young people were milling about, desperately trying to get drunk before closing time.

"How yer goin', mate?" came the familiar voice from the driver of the old Singer Roadster as it drew to a stop.

"I'm here, anyway," Michael responded, hinting at his second thoughts since he'd arrived in Surface Paradise.

After leaving Paradise Avenue, Ralph turned off the macadam and started down a rutted road, drawing up before a big wooden house that was an example of Australian Victorian Gothic architecture. It looked outlandish, like a Chinese pagoda, with its wooden railings upstairs and down. Michael followed Ralph up the sand dune in front of the house and saw the expanse of the South Pacific Ocean under the diffused brightness of the moonlight.

"Mum won't be greetin' ya for dinner, an' she extends her apologies," Ralph announced as they headed back to the house. "She's got one of her migraines."

Entering the house, they were greeted by Mrs. Proctor, a rawboned countrywoman, Mrs. Murchison's housekeeper.

"Like ya ta meet my mate, Mike," Ralph casually announced.

"Pleased ta meetcha!"

"I'm very pleased to make your acquaintance, Mrs. Proctor," Michael said, shaking her hand.

"What's fer tea?" Ralph asked.

"Lamb chops," Mrs. Proctor said before quickly departing.

"Bloody lamb chops!" Ralph groaned, slumping into an armchair beside the fireplace, his leg draped over one arm. "There ya 'ave the acme of Australian culinary art."

Michael remained standing, examining the faded photos and playbills that covered one wall.

"Didn't I ever tell ya that Mum was a celebrated actress on the London stage, famous in 'er time?" Ralph inquired, awaiting a response. "An' that stern-faced old bastard over Mum's desk is me da. It was taken while he was convalescin' during the Second Basho."

Crossing the room, Michael examined the steely-faced colonel with a square jaw and straight shoulders, thinking that Ralph had gotten his physiognomy as well as his temper from his father.

"Mum's like a Limey in thinkin' she's got a social position to keep up," Ralph explained.

Michael sat in the armchair opposite his friend, his face a blank.

"Look, am I borin' ya?"

"I'm sorry, Ralph, it's just that I'm bushed."

"Lemme show ya yer room."

Michael went upstairs to the second floor, toting his suitcase, where Ralph revealed an iron bedstead with a thin mattress and a chest of drawers with a cracked, yellowed mirror. Above the bed was a picture of Anne Hathaway's cottage with an old-fashioned English garden in bloom. Left alone, Michael transferred his clothes to the dresser then washed his face and hands in the washbasin angled into the corner of the room. On his way downstairs, he passed a rubbery plant mounted on an iron stand, the plant reaching out at him with its tentacles.

They sat at a long mahogany table that could accommodate twelve in grander days. The massive mahogany sideboard had the white patina that furniture gets in the tropics.

"My sister was all set ta spend the Christmas hols hiking in Kiwiland, but she's decided ta come 'ome instead," Ralph announced as Michael sat opposite him across the long table.

Mrs. Proctor appeared with the lamb chops, boiled potatoes, and green beans.

"I thought it best ta fill ya in, as I doan' wancha makin' any more of a fool of yerself than ya've done already," Ralph said as Mrs. Proctor left.

Perfectly impassive, Michael looked at Ralph as if he hadn't heard a word he'd said.

"To put matters bluntly, Mum's been livin' beyond 'er means fer years now," Ralph explained. "So now she's got the bright idea of playin' matchmaker. I just thought I'd clue ya in."

Michael put down his knife and fork with a solemn expression. "Ralph, given the circumstances, I'll catch the first train back to Sydney in the morning."

"What's all this to-do 'bout?" Ralph asked, offended. "Didn't I jist give ya fair warnin'? An' remember, my sister doan' know any more than you do."

"I'm sure that when your sister arrives, you'll explain the situation," Michael replied with a hint of sarcasm.

"Look, mate, just leave me sister out of this," Ralph flared angrily. "Gloria's apples! She's a ripper girl!"

"All I said, Ralph, was that I'd be returning to Sydney," Michael protested. "I didn't say anything about your sister. Besides, I hate contrived situations."

"I'm fed up to the back teeth with yer snotty attitude!" Ralph exploded. "That's been yer problem right from the start. My sister's too good fer ya!"

"Please, Ralph, let's drop the tone of personal insult and try to behave in a civilized manner."

Finishing the meal, the two friends sat on the porch, and Michael lit an herbal cigarette.

"Las' year Mum put a fence up the beach to keep the larrikins from Surface Paradise off 'er property," Ralph casually explained.

Michael yawned, wondering why the Murchisons behaved like a medieval baronial family with territory to defend.

"I keep tellin' Mum she ought ta sell this place an' live with Gloria in Sinny, 'cause she doan' 'ave any sorta life 'ere."

"I'm really feelin' bushwacked," Michael protested, standing up.

"Why didn't ya say so?"

"I just did."

"So, are ya goin' ta stay?"

"Lemme sleep on it."

Alone, Michael quickly undressed and lay on his back on the bed. Gratefully, he expanded his lungs and gazed at the ghostly moon beyond the open window. *I can't even remember what Gloria looks like,* Michael thought, *except that her eyes seem to pop out of her head, and she has this bold sort of way of looking at you. First thing in the morning, I'll have to decide about the next train.* As he drew a deep breath, Michael felt that he'd risen from the bed and was drifting out over the South Pacific Ocean.

At eight o'clock the next morning, Michael appeared for breakfast, only to be informed by the taciturn Mrs. Proctor that Mrs. Murchison hoped to join him for dinner that evening and trusted he'd had a good night's rest. Michael asked where Ralph was, and Mrs. Proctor explained that he'd left early to fetch his sister from Southport. Over a solitary breakfast, Michael brooded, wondering why Ralph hadn't arranged for his sister to travel with him, since their journeys were a day apart.

After breakfast Michael nosed about the pictures and playbills in the living room, feeling strangely free from the nagging duties of the American Legation. The thought of Gloria's imminent arrival finally drove him back upstairs to his room, where in the oven-like heat he consulted the timetable to ascertain when the next train departed for Sydney. But having arrived at the end of the world and not yet having met his hostess, he wondered how he could possibly do that.

Standing up, he looked through the open window at the brush-covered sand dune before the house, with the blue-green South Pacific Ocean beyond. The sky was a cloudless blue, and for months at the American Legation he'd been confronted by red-faced Aussies saying that the States offered better opportunities for their cupidity, so he seemed to drift away in the hot, humid air.

Michael felt that he'd earned his fortnight at Surface Paradise despite Gloria's high-minded sense of her own importance. Quickly undressing, he pulled on his swim trunks and his colorful sports shirt featuring a surfer riding an endless wave. With a thin paper Oxford Shakespeare in one hand and a bath towel draped over his shoulder, he tripped lightly downstairs and straight out the front door past the red bougainvillea vine that draped over the porch railing. When he'd climbed to the top of the sand dune, he paused and looked back at the house. His second-floor window was wide open as he'd left it, but the other windows were closed and looked blank and sightless. The house was painted yellow, but it was bleached and faded, looking as if it hadn't been painted in years.

Descending the sand dune, Michael walked halfway to the surf line, where he spread out his towel in the broiling sun, sat down, and began to read *Twelfth Night*:

> *Duke*: If music be the food of love, play on;
> Give me excess of it, that, surfeiting,
> The appetite may sicken, and so die.—
> That strain again!—it had a dying fall:
> O, it came o'er my ear like the sweet south,
> That breathes upon a bank of violets,
> Stealing and giving Odour!—Enough; no more.
> 'Tis not so sweet now as it was before.

After reading a few lines, Michael put the book aside and lay back in the hot sand, closing his eyes. Before him he saw Louis XIV, the Sun King, wearing cloth of gold as he boarded a vessel with the radiant young Mlle. de la Vallière to be transported to the Ile de Cythère.

Suddenly feeling the intensity of the sun, Michael sat up, his eyes falling upon a young woman who was standing by the edge of the sea. She was turned from him, but even as he looked, she turned about in her one-piece bathing suit of pale green that caused a sudden thumping in his heart.

Standing, Michael made a gallant gesture with his right arm, as if he were the Sun King, and said, "What a graceful creature you are! I thought you must be a vision and would suddenly vanish before my eyes!"

"I've just been for a swim," the young woman said, smiling as she pulled her bathing cap off, releasing her dark, flocculent hair, which framed her face in tight curls and rippled when she walked.

"How cruel you are not to invite me," Michael rejoined, still in the guise of the Sun King, for her beauty struck a pain in his heart.

"Would you like to go for a swim?" she asked.

"I'd rather just talk with you."

"Perhaps you'd like to come waterskiing tonight?"

"I would, except that I don't know how."

"Tom'll teach you."

"Tom?"

"My boyfriend."

"Does he let you out of his sight?"

"He can't help it. He's a canecutter near Cairns—but he's comin' tonight."

"Do you know who I am?"

"You're Michael Sykes, Ralph's Yank mate."

"I see. Do you live hereabouts, or do you simply vanish like a sprite?"

"Hasn't Ralph mentioned me? I'm Anne Coleraine, and I live beyond Mrs. Murchison's fence up the beach."

"Does Mrs. Murchison own everything about here?"

"Yes, I'm trespassing! The Old Bat might get me arrested!"

"Not having met the Old Bat, I don't have an opinion."

"Ralph says you're the deep type with your nose always in a book."

"Can we make a pact to always tell each other the truth?" he asked.

"I don't know anything!"

"Tell me everything you've heard then."

"Do you take a fancy to Gloria?" she asked.

"Who told you that?"

"Mrs. Proctor."

"I see," Michael said, laughing at the ludicrousness of the thought.

"I see you're upset, but you shouldn't be. It's Mrs. Murchison who's crazy!"

"So I've heard!"

"She's got ideas about her own importance, and Gloria runs her a close second."

"Why's Ralph so different from his sister?"

"I can't tell you, but last year ..." Anne stopped, thinking it better not to speak.

"Remember our pact?" Michael reminded her.

"Well, last year I worked for Mrs. Murchison, living in the house, but we had a falling out."

"A misunderstanding?"

"Yes."

"About Ralph?"

"Yes, he was sweet on me, but his mother objected. Ralph falls in love with every pretty girl he sees!"

"You didn't love him?"

"You're pretty good at gettin' things outta people, aren't ya?"

"I don't mean to pry. Do you live nearby?"

"Not far. Just up the beach," Anne said. "Our place isn't a palace like the Murchisons'."

"I'd like to see it even if it isn't a palace!"

"To find out how the other half lives?"

"Anne, I don't give a damn about Mrs. Murchison's snobbery!"

"All right. We'll go if you wish."

They started walking up the beach in silence, following the surf line. Dark clouds were forming in the north, moving rapidly to the land.

"How far do we have to go?" Michael asked, turning to look into her brown eyes.

"Let's run for it!" Anne exclaimed, dashing up the wet sand as fleet as Atalanta.

"I can't get my breath!" Michael said, catching up.

"Sissy!"

"Hey, I'm pooped!"

"Are you sick?" Anne asked, stopping and coming back to him.

"No, but I've got asthma."

A sudden bolt of lightning descended from the sky, followed by a thunderclap that reverberated in their chests. Whitecaps were churned up on the sea with a gusty wind that had started blowing with machine-gun-like rain. Anne dashed up the beach and crawled beneath an overturned lifeboat with the prow stoved in. Quickly Michael slipped into the dark, hot space, catching his breath. They lay side by side, listening to the intensity of the rain that beat against the overturned lifeboat above.

"What do you want out of life?" Michael asked, mesmerized by her bright eyes.

"A million quid. That should do me!"

"Wouldn't you rather be a princess in a sleigh on the Steppes, listening to the silver bells on horses' manes?"

"You're a dreamer!"

"I've always wished to live in a world not of my own making," Michael said.

"Storm's over!" Anne exclaimed, quickly crawling out.

"Hey, wait a minute!" he called after her, running to catch up.

After a few minutes, they came to the wooden fence that marked Mrs. Murchison's property line, but it was mostly broken, with the No Trespassing sign lying in the sand.

"The Old Bat used to bring charges against people for trespassin', until she got tired of appearin' in court," Anne explained.

"Maybe she should declare her own country?" Michael suggested with a wry smile.

"She already has!" Anne said, laughing.

Michael followed Anne over the sand dunes and saw the red metal roof of the Coleraines' bungalow, pitched no higher than the surrounding dunes, with a water butt on one side. Anne jumped up onto the wooden porch and opened the front door, with Michael following her into the living room. Immediately he found himself alone in the amber light, for Anne had rustled through the beaded curtain to the back of the bungalow.

A wicker sofa with roses on pink cushions was pushed to one side of the living room, facing a round table with a green cloth and rush mats covering the floor. Bamboo-framed dime-store pictures were on one wall—one of a barefoot boy and girl, the girl in a crinoline dress, and both wearing straw bonnets. Michael thought how his mother would have laughed to see such a picture, as he sat down on the pink floral sofa and stretched out, feeling an infinite sense of languor and contentment.

But suddenly the beaded curtain rattled, and Anne appeared, leading her mother by the hand.

Michael sprang to his feet like a jack-in-the-box.

"So pleased to meetcha, Mr. Sykes," Mrs. Coleraine said, extending her hand. Her voice sounded high-pitched.

"My pleasure, Mrs. Coleraine," Michael replied, shaking her hand, which seemed as delicate as an eggshell. Her eyes were of a perpetual blueness, her hair an impossible red. In a faded floral dress, she looked at him blankly, as if she had been condemned to much suffering.

Mrs. Coleraine sat in the wicker armchair beside the round table, while Anne sat beside Michael on the sofa. Immediately Mrs. Coleraine began rattling off the events of the morning, for she'd just got back from food shopping in Surface Paradise. She didn't like the heat, but it must be endured, though it made her feel tired.

Michael thought that this was a conversation between mother and daughter and noted that Anne had changed into a white sleeveless dress with red hibiscus flowers. Her arms were bare and glowed from the warmth of the sun. Listening to Mrs. Coleraine, he began to feel sleepy and content, just as if he were a member of the family. Mother and daughter started talking about lunch, and Mrs. Coleraine proposed a crayfish salad, which she'd just bought. Michael offered to help, but Anne rejected his plea and went off with her mother to the kitchen, leaving him to stretch out on the sofa, hearing the sound of their voices.

"Sleep well?"

"Oh, I'm terribly sorry!" Michael exclaimed. "Your mother will think me very rude. How long have I slept?"

"It's one o'clock."

"One o'clock! I'd no idea!"

Anne smiled, sitting on the wicker armchair facing him.

"Did you sit there and let me sleep? Your mother will think me a nig-nog!"

"Don't apologize. Do you want to wash up?"

"Just my hands."

Michael followed Anne through the beaded curtain and down the dimly lit hall to the kitchen at the back. "Wash your hands in the sink," she told him.

"Let me clear up first!" Mrs. Coleraine exclaimed, jumping up.

"Stay where you are, Mummy!" Anne said.

"Would Mr. Sykes like a beer?"

"Call me Michael," he insisted. "Yes, I'd love one."

"Sit down, Mummy!" Anne again ordered.

After having drunk only half a bottle of cold Bulimba beer, Michael felt light-headed. "I've got a bungalow right on the beach at Mosman, and I'd like you both to come and live there with me," Michael blurted out. "If that doesn't suit you, I could kip on the porch or find some place close by."

"Can we trust him, Mummy?" Anne asked. "Or is he going to make me his love slave?"

"Anne, I was never more serious about anything in my life!" Michael protested.

"How ever would we repay him?" Mrs. Coleraine asked her daughter, with an expression of vague incomprehension.

"I don't expect to be paid," Michael insisted, taking rapid, shallow breaths.

"Do you think he's got drunk?" Anne asked her mother with a light laugh.

"No, Anne, I'm being very serious!" Michael insisted.

"Well, what do you say, Mummy?" Anne asked. "Shall we take him up on his offer?"

"I do believe he means well," Mrs. Coleraine said.

"I've always wished to live where there are four seasons," Anne announced. "I should especially like to see the snow."

"What would you do in the snow?" Michael asked, mesmerized by her brown eyes, his elbows on the table.

"During a snowstorm, I'd drink champagne in a tree!" Anne responded gleefully.

"How would you get down, if you were tipsy?" Michael asked.

"I'd fall into a six-foot snowdrift!"

"That would be some snowstorm!" Michael exclaimed, laughing.

"Does it snow where you come from in America?"

"Yes, it snows on Long Island."

"Is Long Island someplace in America?"

"Don't they teach geography here?"

"Smarty-pants!"

Smiling, Mrs. Coleraine rose and cut slices of fresh pineapple on the drain board. Michael saw that she looked bright and alert for the first time since he'd met her.

When they'd finished lunch, he insisted on putting on the apron and washing the dishes while the women dried. Afterward, Anne led him back to the living room, producing her photograph album as they sat on the sofa.

"Is that your boyfriend?" Michael asked, seeing them both together.

"Yes, that's Tom Delaney."

"He looks very sure of you."

"Sure of me? I hope so, as much as I am of him!" Anne turned the page. "Here's a snapshot of Tom and me with Robin and Peter at the Cockatoo Bar."

"Is that a river behind you?"

"Yes, the Nerang River, where we go waterskiing," Anne explained.

"I'm dying to kiss you," Michael murmured, putting his arm about her shoulders and kissing her dark hair.

Quickly, Anne turned and pushed him away, but he put his arms about her again and felt the softness of her breasts when a sudden sensation passed through him as their lips met. Overhearing a slamming at the back door, Michael sprang to his feet.

"That's only Mummy goin' to the dunny," Anne assured him. "If Tom knew you'd kissed me, he'd be as mad as a meat axe." Standing behind him, Anne put her arms about his chest.

"I don't care what your boyfriend thinks," Michael protested, turning to look into her sparkling eyes.

"Would you like to dance?" she asked.

"I'm a lousy dancer."

"Don't do me any favors!"

"I'm sorry."

"You don't have to dance if you don't wish to."

"I wish to very much."

Anne knelt beside the round table, took out her portable record player, placed it on the table, and put a record on. The strains of "Charmaine" soon filled the heated air.

"A waltz is just my speed!" Michael said gratefully.

"'Charmaine' is a two-step, duckie."

Michael put his arms about her waist, feeling the softness of her body as they began to shuffle on the rush mat.

"Did your mother ever teach you how to dance?" she asked.

"Believe me, she tried!"

"Tell me something about yourself."

"There's not much to tell."

"I hope you're reasonably ambitious."

"I hope so!"

"Do you wish to become the president of the United States?"

"Why not?"

"You're lucky because you're rich and only have to please yourself."

"Life's not that simple."

"Do you do whatever appeals to you at the moment?"

"You make me sound very selfish!"

"Charmaine" came to an end with a *burr*. Anne lifted the needle and turned off the record player. "I was only saying that if you found yourself unhappy in one particular place, you could go off somewhere else," she said, standing up.

"Everybody's got problems, whether they're rich or not."

"What problem do you have?"

"I've known plenty of rich people who were miserable."

"You've no idea what ordinary people's lives are like."

"Are you angry with me for washing the dishes?" Michael asked, still mesmerized by her bright eyes.

Anne did not respond, so Michael lit another herbal cigarette, looking out the screen door at the hot sand dunes. Stepping close behind him, Anne slipped her hands beneath his shirt, running them up his back to the nape of his neck. "Can I have a puff?"

"You won't like it."

She took the cigarette from him and put it between her lips. "Ugh! How can you smoke such a nasty thing!" Her luminous eyes had shriveled like sea anemones touched with acid.

"They relieve my asthma," Michael explained, opening the screen door and flicking the butt onto the sand dune.

"Do you think I'd like Sydney?" Anne asked, putting her arms about his waist when he'd turned to face her.

"You'd be happy anywhere," Michael assured her. "Is your mother a widow?"

"Daddy was killed in a railroad accident ten years ago," Anne said. "Mummy lives on his pension."

"You could each have a separate bedroom," Michael assured her, possessed by this vision of happiness.

"Do you promise not to sleepwalk?" Anne asked, smiling.

"Honest injun!" Michael replied, slumping onto the sofa and asking himself, *Where is her feminine diffidence? Is Anne as desirable as I think? What about her faithfulness to Tom Delaney?* But these thoughts he quickly pushed aside as unworthy.

"Will you come waterskiin' with us tonight?" she asked him.

"I'd rather be alone with you."

"If Tom sees you pervin' me, he'll do your chump," Anne warned.

"As far as I'm concerned, Tom Delaney doesn't exist."

"He'll be very much in evidence tonight, so you'd better be on your best behavior," Anne cautioned. "Or perhaps you'd rather spend the evening chattin' with Her Grace, the Old Bat?"

"I'd rather be with you."

"Isn't Gloria due today?"

"I don't give a damn about Gloria!"

"If we decide to go, I'll send you word by nine o'clock."

"How will you do that?"

"I dunno, but I'll think of something."

Michael stood up and took hold of her hands. "May I kiss you?"

"Do you always ask a girl if you may kiss her?"

"No, but do you mind?"

"Yes, I *do* mind!" Anne replied, a mocking light in her eyes.

Michael kissed her, but quickly she broke free, passing through the shimmering beaded curtain. Going onto the beach, he climbed the sand dune and started walking southward on the hard, wet sand by the shore.

10

Michael Sykes dawdled down the beach, gazing at the ultramarine of the sea, with great cumulus white clouds above. Thinking of Anne's invitation to go waterskiing with her and her friends, Michael hoped that her ladyship would be indisposed with another migraine. Reaching the Murchisons', he slipped upstairs, encountering no one. Hanging from the hook behind the door was his white cord suit, cleaned and pressed. Immediately he suspected the hand of the hostess, who'd no doubt instructed Mrs. Proctor to have his suit cleaned, which made Michael feel that he was on the slippery slope at the foot of which stood Gloria. Grabbing the big bath towel that had been considerately placed on his bed, he stepped briskly down the hall.

"Mr. Sykes, I've drawn your bath," Mrs. Proctor suddenly announced, appearing from nowhere.

"Thank you very much, Mrs. Proctor!" Michael said, irritated that at every step he found willing hands.

He removed his bathrobe, he lay in the tepid bath with the water up to his nose. *What can have possessed this deluded woman to think she can play matchmaker to her own daughter?* Michael asked himself. *Doubtless that's what comes from living so long in the tropics, for one's mind gets completely out of touch.*

The rest of these ruminations were Michael determining to leave Surface Paradise first thing in the morning. *But what about Anne?*

He caught himself wondering. *What the devil's taken possession of you? You've always managed complications with the opposite sex. If you wish to see Anne, you must inevitably see Gloria ... What the devil are you talking about? Are you besotted with Mrs. Murchison's former housemaid? If you weren't so cowardly, you'd have escaped this morning when you said you were going, but you are determined to see Anne, so you must put steel in your character and face up to the Old Bat, as Anne aptly calls her, a woman who insists on trafficking with her own daughter.*

Michael would have been the first to admit ruefully that his mute soliloquy in the bathtub was a confidence-building technique. Nevertheless, freshly dressed in a cleaned and pressed white cord suit, he tripped lightly down the stairs, praying that Mrs. Murchison might be suffering from another migraine. But that was not to be, for at the bottom of the stairs, Mrs. Murchison was awaiting him, seated on a loveseat with the backdrop of her theatrical memorabilia. Wearing a green silk dress covered with black bugle beads, she greeted him with a radiant smile, her hands clasped in her lap like a pair of white doves. Her eyes were heavily lined with mascara, which contrasted with the delicate whiteness of her skin. Her smile was forced and insincere like that of a brothel madam.

"I fear that my daughter has been delayed again," Mrs. Murchison announced, extending her hand.

"Thank you very much for cleaning my suit. What do I owe you?" Michael rejoined, taking her hand and narrowly escaping falling on her ample bosom, for she gave him a tug.

"Do sit down beside me," Mrs. Murchison urged, patting the cushion beside her. "You owe me nothing, but I do expect Gloria to arrive tomorrow. I hope that you become good friends, as much as I look forward to our opportunity for this tête-à-tête."

"Unfortunately I plan to leave tomorrow," Michael responded stiffly as he sat down.

"I simply won't hear of it!" Mrs. Murchison exclaimed. "I've booked you for a fortnight, so it will be a horror to me if you leave a day sooner. Now that that is settled, what do you wish to drink?"

"A gin and tonic, thank you," Michael replied grimly.

"My husband loved a gin and tonic," Mrs. Murchison said, rising and taking mincing steps to the liquor cabinet, for her dress was too tight.

Feeling intimidated by Mrs. Murchison's gentle, if resolute manner, Michael was determined to give her as little insight as possible into the state of his own feelings. He lit an herbal cigarette, struck by the elegant presence and melodious voice of the former celebrated actress of the London stage. Her luxuriant chestnut hair was streaked with gray, and she wore it dramatically swept up into a bun at the back of her head. On her left finger was an enormous ring that looked unreal.

"Gloria has decided to fly to Coolangatta in the morning," Mrs. Murchison explained as she handed him his drink, while sipping a sweet sherry. "Did you manage to lunch today?"

"No, but I got too much sun!" Michael replied, taken aback by her directness. "Do you expect Ralph back tonight?"

"He'll be staying at Coolangatta to pick up Gloria in the morning."

Mrs. Proctor appeared to announce dinner.

"I haven't had a gentleman take me to dinner in some years!" Mrs. Murchison exclaimed, a smile on her lips as she stood. "I feel that I'm again on the London stage!"

"Glad to be of service," Michael responded, blushing.

Dinner offered no concession to the tropics; it consisted of roast beef, Yorkshire pudding, boiled potatoes, and string beans. During the meal, Mrs. Murchison reminisced on her early married life as a grazier's wife, with the annual meeting of the Graziers' Association being the big yearly event. The grazier families entertained each other occasionally and were seemingly oblivious of the great distance that separated their remote sheep stations.

She confessed she'd never adjusted to life in Australia and wished to have her children educated in England. But that was not agreeable to her husband, so she'd suffered the indignity of seeing her son's speech corrupted by roustabouts. Once her sister-in-law had visited them at Boonderoo and brought ponies for the children: a bay mare for Ralph and a chestnut pony for Gloria. The children would think nothing of going off wherever they liked, for Boonderoo comprised ten thousand acres. Of course there was the danger of snakes, but her husband insisted that the children learn the lore of the Bush, so she felt she'd lost them, although her husband insisted that children were easily bored and their lives shouldn't be too regulated.

Michael felt that Mrs. Murchison had made an insufficient effort to adjust to Australian life, but he didn't tell her so, for he was surprised by her reaction when he'd told her of a parade he'd seen on one of his first days in Australia. Mounted on a float was a figure of Britannia with a banner that said *England's Strength Rests in the Bible.*

"Everywhere I go in Australia I find war memorials in townships commemorating wars that weren't of your own making," Michael said. "It struck me as incongruous that with the yellow wattle in bloom you should emphasize dying for England."

"You had your revolution and found new ways of doing things, but in Australia it's different," Mrs. Murchison explained. "England is *home* to us, and we've fought for England because England is always right, no matter how foolish she may be, like a scatterbrained old lady on the tram who insists she's been insulted. When the war was started in Thirty-Nine, it meant that Australia must fight too, even though my husband claimed that Churchill had stabbed us in the back by giving Russia the fighter planes that were needed to defend Singapore."

Mrs. Murchison rose and returned with a book. "This volume is about the Australian Seventh Division in which my husband served. They fought in North Africa at Tobruk, then in New Guinea after Prime Minister Curtin countermanded Churchill's order and brought our troops home to defend Australia."

Michael began turning the pages of the book.

"You're a very charming young man!" Mrs. Murchison suddenly exclaimed.

Michael looked askance at his hostess, blushing as he lay the book aside. "Don't you regret giving up the stage?"

"I flattered myself that I might become another Sarah Bernhardt!" Mrs. Murchison said. "But I was fluttered by a dashing Colonel Murchison, gave up becoming a celebrated actress, and married a grazier, living in the back of the beyond."

"That must have been quite a cultural shock for you after London?"

"A sheep station is not a school of manners!" Mrs. Murchison said. "But after ten years of finding myself in the middle of nowhere, I moved to Surface Paradise and bought this house."

"What's Boonderoo like now?" Michael asked.

"The station house is in ruins," Mrs. Murchison explained, "but when I lived there it was the first age of the world, when we tended flocks. My husband's grandfather built the station house, consisting of but one room, which became the kitchen. Later the original dwelling was expanded with two wings."

"When I first arrived in Australia, I felt I'd dropped off the edge of the world," Michael confessed. "It was a place unconnected with any other place, because every other place seemed so very far away. I remember standing on the Pylon Lookout on Sydney Harbor Bridge and seeing the sign that shows how far away all the major cities of the world are. I really don't know how I'd have gotten out of my mood of disconnectedness if I hadn't met Ralph, who gave me a kick in the pants and brought me to my senses."

"Ralph is the person who will do that!" Mrs. Murchison said, laughing.

"Too right!" Michael exclaimed as if he were an Aussie.

"Australia has always claimed Ralph for her own, but with Gloria it is different," Mrs. Murchison said. "She appreciates things that the typical Australian has no time for. That's why I wished to have her properly educated, even though my husband was opposed to it when I sent her to the Church of England grammar school at Tenterfield, just over the border in New South Wales. Then she got her degree in journalism from Macquarie University in Sydney. You see, Gloria and I have a relationship that is based on perfect candor. She knows that I want what is best for her, which means she always puts forth her best effort."

Suddenly Mrs. Proctor appeared to announce, "A letter for Mr. Sykes."

"A letter at this hour?" Mrs. Murchison asked, knitting her brows.

"Brought by Peter Lutchford," Mrs. Proctor said. "Perhaps you heard the racket of his Land Rover?"

"Thank you!" Michael exclaimed, jumping to his feet and taking the letter, quickly noting the lateness of the hour. "Mrs. Murchison, I got far too much sun today, and my head is spinning."

"Let me get you a Beecham's Powder and some lemon juice," Mrs. Murchison insisted, rising. "I'll bring it straight up to your room."

"That won't be necessary, Mrs. Murchison," Michael said. "In half an hour, I'll be sleeping like a top and awake completely refreshed in the morning."

"I'm exactly the same," Mrs. Murchison said. "But I never fall asleep without reading a whodunit."

"Good night. I'll have *The History of the Seventh Australian Division* to get started on," Michael replied, picking up the book.

"Mrs. Proctor, please don't stand gawking!" Mrs. Murchison admonished her housekeeper.

Reaching his room, Michael ripped open Anne's letter, which was written in haste, in red pencil.

8 o'clock

Dear Michael,

Tom's finally arrived and we'll be going waterskiing tonight. We'll wait for you till nine—unless you'd rather chat with the Old Bat? Peter will deliver this; perhaps you can come back with him? Please don't worry. I've muzzled Tom, so he won't bite you!

Ya cobber, in haste,
Anne

Quickly Michael put on his swimsuit, pulling his pants over them. He thrust Anne's letter into the pocket. He put on his shoes, for a moment staring at the floorboards, asking himself if it would be too much bother to go up the beach to be with Anne and her friends. Hadn't he seen enough of Aussies on the piss, when even his most innocuous comment could be misconstrued into leading to a punchup?

What the devil are you talking about? Michael suddenly asked himself. *You'd walk on live coals or commit murder just to be with Anne tonight!*

11

Opening the bedroom door, Michael listened. Everything was quiet, so he flitted to the landing, where the rubber plant reached out its snakelike tendrils. He descended wraithlike to the front door, which was diffused in the brightness of moonlight. Reaching the top of the sand dune, he paused and looked back at the house. A bedroom light was lit on the second floor on the left side of the house. *Probably Mrs. Murchison*, he thought, *reading her whodunit.*

When he reached the beach, he ran fast along the hard, flat sand by the shore, running faster than he thought he should have, for his lungs were about to burst. Shortly after slackening his pace, he reached the property line and climbed up the brush-covered sand dune, looking about for Anne's bungalow. A moment later he heard their voices, with Anne's voice sounding silvery with laughter against the background of deep male voices, like an aria being sung that lifts the spirit like a bird rising from the earth. Stumbling down the next sand dune, Michael saw the dark figures on the porch silhouetted against the light of the bungalow, and he ran forward.

"Michael's here!" Anne's voice rang out. She jumped from the porch and ran across the sand dune, grabbing his hand and leading him back to the porch as if he were her latest triumph, like winning last year's Surface Paradise beauty pageant.

"This is my boyfriend, Tom Delaney," Anne said to Michael, as the canecutter leaned against the rail.

"Pleased to meet you, Tom," Michael said, putting out his hand.

"Same 'ere, mate," Tom said, crunching Michael's knuckles as he asked Anne, "Yer friend a Pom?"

"No, Michael's a Yank."

"Got yer bather on, Mike?" Tom asked, looking amused.

"Yes, under my pants," Michael said.

"We've had a change of plans," Anne explained. "We're not goin' waterskiing."

"Doancha know it ain't safe to go waterskiin' after dark?" Tom asked Michael.

"Tom's just back from the Bush, so he wants to get boozed," Anne said.

"If we doan' look slippy, we won't 'ave enough time to get pissed," Tom warned.

"If you're going to get drunk, you can count me out," a woman with them announced.

"Michael, this is Robin Bowles—Robin, Michael," Anne said.

"Pleased to meet you," Michael responded, shaking Robin's hand and noticing how blonde her hair was.

"An' this is her boyfriend, Peter Lutchford," Anne said.

"'Ow's it goin', mate?" Peter asked, thrusting his hand at Michael.

"Hi, Peter!" Michael said, seeing that Peter was blond too, so that the two might pass for brother and sister, except for the fact that they clung to each other as if each shared his better self in the other. There was a frank openness about them that nothing could hide, as if the difference in sex was no more than an anatomical one.

Anne thrust a cold tinnie into Michael's hand, taking him aside, saying, "Isn't Tom a cutie?"

"He's a yobbo!" Michael whispered.

"'Ere, what's all this about?" Tom asked, having overheard.

Anne flew to Tom's side, putting her arms around his waist.

"More like me girl," Tom grunted, appeased for the moment. "She attracts men like the flowers do bees." Tom threw this observation out for anyone who cared to listen.

As he drank his beer, Michael looked at Tom, but even in the weak light he looked like a statue of a pagan god; his powerful, bronzed body was in superb condition. But he was as inarticulate as a statue too, which grated on Michael, for when he looked into Tom's eyes, he felt he was looking into the dead heart of Australia. Maybe Tom even had a touch of Abo blood, for he had a long face and a straight nose, with his hair straight and black, almost covering his ears.

"Come inside, Michael, and take off your trunks," Anne urged, taking his hand.

"Gimme a moment," Michael said, his head spinning.

"Take yer time, mate, yer in good 'ands," Peter advised, guffawing.

He stepped into the parlor after Anne and followed her through the rattling beaded curtain down the hall to her bedroom, where she switched on the dresser table lamp.

"Just gimme a minute," Michael said, embarrassed at being in her bedroom.

Smiling at him with her bright eyes, Anne left, closing the door.

Quickly Michael took off his white cord pants and pulled down his damp swimsuit, with Tom Delaney's face still before his eyes, the wide lips cracked in a sneer and fissured like a creek bed in a drought. His dark suit was doubtless Sunday best, although it didn't fit properly, for his big wrists protruded from the sleeves, and the fabric was too tightly stretched across his broad shoulders.

When Michael returned to the porch, they all walked to the back of the bungalow and climbed into Peter Lutchford's Land Rover, which jounced over the unsealed path to the macadam road, where Peter opened her up, with the swirling of white moths churning like a snowstorm in the headlights. Beside the road he could see the gum trees standing like naked people in the night. Robin sat up front beside Peter while Anne was in the backseat, sandwiched between Michael and her boyfriend. In the darkness, Michael felt her thigh pressed against his, wondering if she did it on purpose as a secret sign of her encouragement or because of the movement of the vehicle. For some time he hadn't been able to draw a deep breath.

Half an hour later Peter Lutchford drew up before a sputtering red neon sign on the rooftop of a wooden building that read Cockatoo Bar. Once outside the car, Michael lagged behind, noting that the bar was built on pilings above the river. Looking up, he saw myriad stars in the black sky, visible despite the moon, and wondered if the Creator had taken a perverse delight in such a display, knowing that His handiwork would not be visible to many mortals in the Southern Hemisphere.

Michael entered the bar and went to the men's room, where a tall, skinny youth was peering into the mirror above the washbasin, popping blackheads. The urinal being right there, Michael, wishing to make no gratuitous display of his manhood, slipped into the toilet and bolted the door. When he heard the youth leave, he flushed the toilet with his foot before trying to slide the bolt, which refused to budge, no matter how hard he hit it with the heel of his hand.

After deciding he must climb over the top of the door, Michael saw that there was scant space there, but managed to hoist himself up and hang precipitously between the top of the door and the ceiling, with one leg over, so that he couldn't retreat. The floor seemed to rise toward him, making him feel dizzy, and he recollected, as a small boy, seeing a newly hatched bird futilely trying to peck its way out of its shell. So he'd cracked the shell, freeing the gangling wet hatchling, which he'd left beneath a hedge, wondering what its fate would be. Finally, Michael jumped to the floor.

The band was playing "Surabaya Johnny" as Michael skirted the dance floor and sat opposite Anne and her friends at a table above the Nerang River.

"Does your friend drink plonk, like they do in Paddo?" Tom asked Anne, erupting into hyenic laughter.

"You'd 'ave to be cuttin' cane too long up North like this joker to appreciate Tom's sense of humor," Anne advised Michael.

"This dingbat 'ere thought we wuz goin' waterskiin' ta-night," Tom needlessly explained to Robin and Peter.

Everyone laughed, as if there were no end to this joke. *Perhaps there was,* Michael thought, *if your brains had been fried cutting cane?*

"Well, we'll see whatcha can do surfin' sumtime," Tom informed Michael.

"Michael's better at dancing," Anne advised, smiling at him.

"It's my shout; I'm buyin'!" Michael announced, seeing the waitress.

* * *

When he'd drunk his bottle of Bulimba beer, Michael immediately felt that his brains had been fried too. Anne was still clinging to Tom's side as close as an orchid clings to the rough bark of a jungle tree, an epiphyte drawing its sustenance from the air. In her eyes was the bright sparkle of excitement and on her skin the light patina of perspiration.

"I've never gone surfin'," Michael said.

"It's great ta ride down the wall with the soup curlin' behind ya," Peter said to Michael.

"Peter's won many surfin' contests," Robin told Michael.

Michael jerked his leg, suddenly realizing that Anne had stroked him with her foot, her eyes telling him that she was drawn to him, though she must conciliate Tom.

As he lit an herbal cigarette, Michael blew the smoke above his head.

"They stink!" Robin cried.

"He smokes 'em for his asthma," Anne explained.

"What's it like cutting cane?" Michael asked Tom.

"It's hard yakka, mate," Tom conceded. "Besides, we 'ave a snake in the cane fields what's called a taipan, an' if yer bit, yer a dead man when the poison reaches yer 'eart. Once't I seen a bloke whot got bit by a taipan, an' he run 'bout like a hairy goat, but in a minute it wuz all up wi' 'im."

"Isn't there a remedy against this snake?" Michael asked.

"No, nothin'. Whatcha 'ave to do is cut yer finger off as quick as a wink." Tom advised, making a karate chop with his hand on the table.

"I hope we've found something more pleasant to talk about when we return," Robin protested, going off with her boyfriend to dance.

"Tom, let's forget about snakes," Anne urged. "Michael, would you like to dance?"

"Yeah, sure!" Michael replied, feeling uneasy but smiling at her sudden transition. Anne kissed Tom's cheek, assuring him he'd have the next dance. But to Michael it was almost as if she were telling Tom that she didn't want to be with him anymore and that he himself would have to find the courage to stand up to him.

They began dancing, and Michael felt that he never wanted to let Anne go. She danced instinctively to the tempo of the moment, so the music was irrelevant. Her eyes were those of a lover. It seemed to Michael that it had been so sudden; she was warm and soft, and he wished to possess her like an animal.

When the dance ended, Michael insisted they go outside, which she agreed to without a word being spoken. They walked down the gangway to the dock, where the moon shone on the Nerang River. Anne was beautiful in the moonlight, her eyes shining on him steadily. Silence grew between them as if they were in the jungle, hearing the strains of an exotic dance—the dance that she should have had with Tom Delaney.

"Clearly, Tom resents you, so don't allow yourself to be intimidated," Anne urged.

"Your boyfriend won't bully me," Michael insisted.

"You don't know Tom. He is very kind and sincere."

"But you don't love him anymore."

"No, I don't."

"Anne, I love you," Michael replied. "Long before I met you, I knew I'd find you. Do you love me?"

"Yes, I do. Why don't you kiss me? Or are you going to ask my permission?"

"Yes," Michael muttered, taking her into his arms and lifting her into the air, all the imaginary barriers in his mind having given way. He was stunned by the ardor of her response. All his life had been a journey in which he'd been hidden from himself. She was joy, the sound of laughter, with the world locked away. Feeling her soft breasts, he kissed the hollow of her neck, smelling the perfume that tasted like the salt of the sea. Already they were on their desert caravan, laden with silks and precious jewels. That night they would bathe beneath a palm in an oasis, lying in each other's arms and watching the myriad stars. The softness of her kiss brought a numbness to his brain and senses. How beautiful she was, and how beautiful their children would be.

"Anne! Mike! Tom's done 'is block!" Peter's voice rang out in the sudden darkness.

Anne screamed, breaking free of Michael, her face an expressionless mask. At first Michael had no idea what was happening, for Peter had tried to pacify Tom, telling him that he had no reason to be alarmed. But Tom quickly came to his senses, explaining that he must get his girl, so he began moving steadily toward the door. Peter had dashed ahead of him, calling to Anne and Michael, but he'd turned to block Tom to no avail, for he'd picked him up and thrown him into the Nerang River. Michael looked bemused, as if he were far away.

Tom's first punch was to the stomach, the second to the jaw, sending Michael sprawling to the dock. Anne screamed, while Peter climbed from the river and sprang onto Tom's back, riding him like a horse before being catapulted again into the river. Then Tom stood over Michael, who was seated on the dock, holding his jaw. For a moment Tom muttered to himself, but when Anne screamed again, he blindly strode up the gangway into the darkness.

"Let's go home!" Robin cried, suddenly appearing.

"I wish you'd given 'im one good punch!" Anne cried to Michael.

"The poor bastard doan' know his own strength," Michael said, pulling himself to his feet. Even in the moonlight you could see the blood on his jacket. "What about Tom? How's he goin' to get home?"

"You won't see Tom again tonight," Peter said, having climbed a second time from the river.

"If you make up with Tom, I'll never speak to you again!" Anne wailed at Michael.

"Whaddaya mean? I just know how he feels," Michael insisted.

On the drive back to Surface Paradise, Peter was asking himself why the course of young love with Robin should have been nothing but habitual bickering. Some of their friends had told them that they shouldn't have gone steady for so long. Or maybe Fate had dealt them a deck without the Queen of Hearts? But it was just maddening for their friends to have to watch them.

Peter drew up the Land Rover a few yards before Anne's bungalow and switched off the headlights. Anne had been crying, but she got out with Michael, and they walked with their arms about each other to the bungalow. When Peter switched on the headlights, he caught them kissing.

Then Peter dropped Michael off at the Murchisons' before heading down the unsealed path to the macadam road, where he pulled over to the verge and switched off the headlights.

"Why are we stopping?" Robin asked.

"Stop pretendin' ya doan' know!" Peter snapped.

"Whenever we go on a date, you act like a beast!" Robin cried.

"Why are ya holdin' back?" Peter asked, his voice plaintive.

"I've told you why!" Robin protested. "When the time's right, I won't hold back."

"After we're married, ya mean?"

"Yes—after I've finished nurse's training."

"Oh, oreright."

"I know it's frustrating for you, but why must you prove yourself?"

"Don't act narky. I said I'm sorry."

Peter put his arms about Robin and they kissed, but in the darkness he could see the Yank madly kissing Anne.

Alone in his room, Michael stretched out naked on the bed and began reading *The History of the Australian Seventh Division*. "These men have not died in vain," so began the words of the divisional chaplain at a memorial service at the end of the war. "They will live again in our memory and in lives made better because of their sacrifice."

Michael tossed the book aside and got up to switch off the light. *Strange*, he thought, lying on his stomach on the bed, *to be reading about death and suffering when all I can think about is Anne.*

12

Michael opened his eyes the following morning and saw that a letter had been thrust beneath his door. Springing from the bed, he seized it and tore the envelope open.

5 a.m.

Dear Michael,

I'm leaving in a few minutes with Tom Delaney to stay with his parents at Cairns. Last night left my head spinning. I know I've hurt Tom, never meaning to do so because we have a very special love as has become only too obvious to me, for we were meant for each other. I entertain no romantic thoughts about you, which is not to say that I don't respect and admire you for being what you are. But we are two different people, although I am grateful to you for offering to help my mummy and me, but our problems are our own.

Under different circumstances, I might have felt different, but you will think my "woman's reasons" vain. But I do not regret having known you, however briefly.

No, I must haste!

Ya cobber,
Anne

Reading between the lines, Michael assured himself, *She's fearful. Doubtless Tom put undue pressure on her. But she'd drop Tom if she weren't afraid of him.* Folding the letter, Michael thrust it back into the envelope, determined to go up the beach to speak with her, and if she'd already left, he'd get Tom's Cairns address from Mrs. Coleraine. Not bothering to shave, he dressed quickly in his cord suit and tore downstairs, only to encounter Ralph and his sister at the bottom. Gloria looked remarkably fresh despite the overnight train journey from Sydney—if she hadn't flown to Coolangatta. Dressed in a tan, smartly tailored suit with a silk blouse and cameo at the throat, she looked conspicuously chic.

"I won't be having breakfast—hello, Gloria!" Michael blurted out.

"Whoa! Why the big hurry?" Ralph interjected, grabbing his friend by the arm. "You must at least act sociable—like the rest of us!"

Gloria gave Michael a hypocritical smile, saying, "I stopped at the American Legation yesterday and picked up some letters for my brother and a Christmas card for you."

"An old flame from the States, I expect?" Ralph surmised, guiding Michael into the dining room, where Mrs. Murchison was seated at the head of the table.

"Oh, Gloria, it's lovely to see you!" Mrs. Murchison said in greeting, rising to kiss her daughter's forehead.

Michael faced Gloria at the center of the table, while Ralph sat at the opposite end from his mother. No sooner were they all seated than Mrs. Proctor served grapefruit, which made Michael's mouth wince.

"How'd ya come ta split yer lip, mate?" Ralph asked Michael.

"I seem to have walked into the door in the dark," Michael replied, blushing.

"That isn't what the little bird said!" Gloria exclaimed, laughing.

"Ain't they just like Beatrice an' Benedict?" Ralph observed to his mother. "Wouldn't ya think they'd be sayin' 'ow 'appy they were ta see each other?"

"Oh, I'm very pleased to see Gloria," Michael said.

"As pleased as I am to see you again, Michael, I'm sure," Gloria responded in her cool manner.

"Now ain't that nice, almost lovey-dovey, I'd say," Ralph interjected.

"What do you propose doing to enliven things?" Gloria asked Michael, ignoring her brother. "Surface Paradise is really quite dull. Nobody comes here that anyone wishes to see. I had planned my holiday in New Zealand, spending a fortnight in Fjordland and hitchhiking with a small group on Stewart Island, which I believe is the sole place where you can see the native kiwi bird."

"Anytime, ya can see a lot of kiwis in Sinny," Ralph observed, smiling at his wretched pun.

"As I was saying, before my brother rudely interrupted me," Gloria said, "I can't imagine why anyone comes to Surface Paradise. The heat is perfectly appalling, but then I suppose if you wish to become inebriated or laze on the beach?"

"My son tells me, Michael, that you enjoy bushwalking," Mrs. Murchison said, wishing to change the subject of conversation.

"Yes, last Christmas I bushwalked in the Blue Mountains," Michael said. "I started from Wentworth Falls without an adequate map and soon became lost, but I bumped into another bushwalker who set me straight. I felt like a nig-nog."

"Oh, that can happen to anyone," Gloria assured Michael, smiling. "Ralph says you stayed at the Jenolan Caves in the Blue Mountains?"

"Yeah, I spent three nights there and couldn't tell a stalactite from a stalagmite!" Michael said.

"Weren't the lights in the caverns like fairyland?" Gloria asked Michael.

"If yer lookin' fer fairyland, go to Paddo on Saturday night," Ralph said, guffawing.

"Do forgive my brother," Gloria told Michael. "He's never civil with the opposite sex."

"That's right. Breedin's a waste of time on a yobbo like me," Ralph assured Michael with a wink.

"My brother makes me regret not having had my holiday in New Zealand this year!" Gloria exclaimed, magnifying her own sense of exasperation. "Tell me, Michael, have you traveled a great deal in Europe?"

"Not since I was a kid," Michael replied. "My parents went there every summer."

"I do envy you!" Gloria said. "Europe has so many cultural advantages. Don't you just love to travel in Europe?"

"No. Actually, I prefer Australia," Michael said, "even though I knew nothing about the country before I came here."

"Well, our Australian climate is dreadfully hot and dry and turns the skin to leather," Mrs. Murchison said. "I avoid the heat of the sun as much as possible."

"I won't 'ear a word said 'gainst Oz!" Ralph protested. "Mum, Oz is the best damn country in the world!"

"What do you base your comparison on, since you've never been out of Australia?" Gloria challenged her brother.

"No more'n you 'ave," Ralph replied. "It gets me ticked off when people start sayin' that Europe's too lovely for words. Doan' act as if this country ain't good enough fer ya, when yer not got enough fer it!"

"Actually, I'm very proud to be an Australian," Gloria assured Michael, ignoring her brother. "Australian men believe they're betraying their origins if one takes the least interest in cultural matters, but women find it easier to adapt."

"What plans do you have for today?" Mrs. Murchison asked, steering the conversation away from dangerous ground.

"This morning, I've an article to write," Gloria announced. "This afternoon you shall find me lazing on the beach."

"And what plans do the young men have?" Mrs. Murchison asked.

"Mike doan' know it yet, but he goin' ta help me get the *Sea Lark* ready for the water—ain't ya, Mike?" Ralph said.

"As you are perhaps aware, my brother is suicidal," Gloria said to Michael. "He'll sail into the teeth of a cyclone."

"Gloria makes me out a dill!" Ralph protested.

"Have you ever noticed that when my brother resorts to his bullocky language, he's invariably wrong?"

"I certainly objected to my husband's language," Mrs. Murchison professed, "for I always said it was excessively strong."

"It wasn't Daddy's language that you objected to," Gloria reminded her mother.

"That may be true, my dear, but a gentleman shouldn't speak like a navvy," Mrs. Murchison insisted.

"What if I took Mike back to the States in the *Sea Lark*?" Ralph suggested.

"Brother, I trust that is a joke!" Gloria said with alarm.

"Well, as far as I can see, life's a game of two-up," Ralph philosophized. "Dicey, ain't it, 'cause one never knows when one's time's up?"

"I object to the fatalism of the Australian male," Gloria remarked, looking into Michael's eyes.

"But I ain't stuck with it?" Ralph replied. "As far as I can see, the blokes do the yakka, leavin' wimmen ta natter, clean 'ouse, an' change nappies."

"What a profound piece of philosophical wisdom!" Gloria announced, standing up. "I bid you gentlemen good morning! Perhaps I'll have the pleasure of seeing you both on the beach, or do you have other plans?"

"Mike's got no plans, 'cept ta help me caulk the *Sea Lark*," Ralph assured his sister. "He's signed on fer the fortnight, and I'll see that he sticks to his bargain."

"Then I hope to see you both this afternoon," Gloria announced.

Michael dragged himself to his feet, and Ralph followed his example.

13

Michael went straight to his room after breakfast and quickly changed into his khaki shorts and white T-shirt. He thrust his bare feet into leather sandals and cinched them. After rereading Anne's letter, he went downstairs and left the house. When he reached the top of the sand dune, he turned to look back at the house, for he saw a shadowed figure standing behind the gauzy curtain on the second-floor window. He thought it was Mrs. Murchison, but wasn't sure, so he turned away and walked down the sand dune to the hard, wet sand on the shoreline.

As he set off in a northerly direction under the blazing sun, the perspiration began trickling from his scalp down his face. When he reached the overturned lifeboat with the stoved-in prow, he sheltered beneath it as he had done the previous day with Anne, not to avoid a thunderstorm but to avoid the intense rays of the sun and read Jaine's Christmas card, which contained a letter.

New York
December 8, 195—

Dear Michael,

I haven't heard a peep out of you in more than a month and have been wondering if you'd fallen off the edge of the world, as you feared you might.

Or have you started to live life to the hilt and wish to be left alone?

Last time I wrote, I didn't tell you that I thought I was pregnant, but it proved a false alarm, so it's not to be. So this good little pampered wife is still finding life so difficult, while you are still going about the world as your old dispassionate self. Or have you found that "someone special" whom you've been looking for?

Are you now deeply bronzed and sporting a beard, like Bluebeard? I think of you fondly—often! So do write and put me out of my misery of having "no news."

I send you a special Christmas kiss—three of them!

XXX
Love from
Jaine

Michael folded the sheet of thin paper, placed it inside her Christmas card, then put it in the envelope, which he had placed in his back pocket. Continuing up the beach, he reached the broken wooden fence that marked the northern limit of Mrs. Murchison's domain. He climbed the sand dune and saw Mrs. Coleraine's bungalow shimmering in the hot sun, the water butt beside the red tin roof, the place looking insubstantial in the undulating hot air. His head was splitting with a fierce headache as he descended the sand dune and sprang onto the porch.

Tapping lightly on the screen door, he peered into the dimly lit living room, but got no response. So he sat down on the steps, his legs in the sun as he hunched over, holding his splitting head. Hearing the screen door creak behind him, he looked up to see Mrs. Coleraine wearing the same floral print dress she'd worn the day before, her face pale and abstracted, with a quizzical, pleading expression, as if life had been too much for her and she didn't understand why people did what they did.

Michael stood up and turned about. "I've come to speak with Anne."

"Didn't she say she'd gone to Cairns with her boyfriend?" Mrs. Coleraine asked, her voice flatly metallic.

"Do you know when she's comin' back?"

"In a fortnight, I think."

"I won't be here then. Can I have Mr. Delaney's address in Cairns—an' if you have his phone number, I'll have that too, as I'll be goin' up there."

"Will you?" Mrs. Coleraine asked with a weak smile—a smile that almost sympathized with his plight.

"Look, I've got a crackin' headache. Could I have an aspirin?" Michael asked.

"It's the sun," Mrs. Coleraine explained as she pushed open the screen door. "Come sit in the parlor while I get you one."

"Thank you, Mrs. Coleraine," Michael replied, stepping into the amber light and slumping onto the bamboo sofa with its cushions adorned with pink roses. Hunching over, his head throbbing, Michael pressed the heels of his hands into his eye sockets.

After a few minutes, he heard the clicking of the beaded curtain and looked up to see Mrs. Coleraine standing before him, a sweet smile on her face like a solicitous mother, holding a glass in one hand and the small white pill in the other. Michael put the aspirin in his mouth, then drank most of the cool glass of water. Her smile had ended his impression of the previous day, when he'd thought she seemed vague, only the shadow of a person.

"I don't think you have a fever," Mrs. Coleraine announced, placing her right hand on his forehead.

"Mrs. Coleraine, I'd like to come here every day," Michael protested.

"That would be nice," Mrs. Coleraine said as she sat down on the wicker armchair beside the circular table matching the sofa. "You might come for tea, if you wished."

"Would you let me have Tom Delaney's address in Cairns?" Michael asked, his eyes falling on the dime-store pictures above the desk of the barefooted girl and boy, where in one picture they were walking down a dusty road on a hot summer day going fishing, for they had fishing poles over their shoulders. The little parlor seemed to breathe Anne's presence, so that he'd never been so happy and content at any time in his life before.

"I shouldn't, but I will," Mrs. Coleraine said, getting up and taking the address book from beside the King James Bible on the shelf above the desk and writing Tom's address on a scrap of notepaper.

"I'm crazy 'bout Anne and wanna marry her," Michael blurted out as he took the slip of paper from Mrs. Coleraine. "What I said yesterday I meant from the bottom of my heart. You can both come and live with me in Sydney."

"Oh, I don't know," Mrs. Coleraine said, looking doubtful, as if she should be offended.

"When I get back from Cairns, do you object to my staying here?" Michael pressed. "I wouldn't be a bother, and I could kip on the sofa, or on the floor for that matter."

"That would be nice, if Anne thinks it's best," Mrs. Coleraine responded as if she had no moral support, since her husband had been killed in that railroad accident ten years before. Living on a pension for all those years, she hadn't expected a stranger to come and make such an outlandish proposal. *Could he be mocking my poverty?* Mrs. Coleraine asked herself. *Or has he just had too much sun?*

"My bungalow in Mosman is right across the road from the beach, so you'll both feel right at home," Michael said, possessed by the vision of his happy future with Anne, even if he had to provide for her mother as well.

"That sounds nice," she allowed, vaguely suspicious.

"D'ya know yesterday when I first met Anne and she brought me back here, I felt I could stay in this bungalow forever," he said, speaking as one mesmerized.

"Did you?" she responded, as if she didn't understand.

"Tell me about Anne. What kind of child was she?"

"A reg'lar tartar she was, from the time she was born," Mrs. Coleraine said, more animated, as if she were looking into a mirror reflection of the past. "She had those eyes of hers that were bold as brass. Ever she were like that—and so were George."

"George?"

"Me firstborn, before my husband went to work for the railroad. At first he cow-cockeyed, for not long after we were married, his father died and left him his farm near Repentance Creek."

"What's cow-cockeying?" Michael asked.

"Dairy farmin' in a small way. It were no easy life, and my husband didn't know that much 'bout it, even though he were born there, but takin' no interest in it till he married me. We tried keepin' the place as best we could, but the water tank always needed repairin' an' if it weren't that, the water pump always needed fixin'. We couldn't afford 'elp an' at night we'd 'ear weird noises."

"What noises?"

"'Ave ya ever 'eard a chook bein' killed by a carpet snake?" Mrs. Coleraine asked.

"Do snakes kill chickens?"

"Yes, the carpet snake does. Me 'usband caught 'im the next mornin' and banged 'im on the head with a shovel. But that weren't 'alf of it: dingoes slaughtered the ducks, and our goats got paralyzed with ticks. Repentance Creek tore our 'earts out, after the five years we'd tried to make a go of it. Then tragedy struck and neither of us 'ad the 'eart to go on, so we left."

"Did something happen to George?"

"Yes, we told him never to go under the house, which were built on stilts, as 'ouses are in Queensland. But 'ow are ya goin' to keep a boy from mischief? One day George come runnin' from beneath the 'ouse, screamin' 'is 'ead off like a banshee."

"What had happened to him?"

"He'd been bit by a black snake. The poor boy died in my arms before we could get 'im to the 'ospital, which was thirty miles off on a bumpy road. After our son died, we left cow-cockeyin' fer good an' me 'usband took 'is job with Queensland Railroad, where he became a signals inspector."

Mrs. Coleraine sat up straight and began smoothing her dress with the palms of her hands, as if she were ironing. Michael hunched over, his hands over his eyes.

"'Ow 'bout something for lunch?" Mrs. Coleraine suddenly asked, standing. "I've got some crayfish left. Do ya fancy a crayfish salad?"

"I'm crazy about crayfish!" Michael exclaimed, jumping up when she did.

"An' as for my daughter, don't worry 'bout her, 'cause she won't marry without my permission," Mrs. Coleraine affirmed.

"I'm crazy about Anne! Whatever happens to me now, at least I'll know that once I was happy."

"Oh?" Mrs. Coleraine said, looking surprised.

"Let me help you with lunch!" Michael pushed through the beaded curtain after her.

14

Wearing a black silk dress with a mantilla of black Spanish lace about her shoulders, Mrs. Murchison descended onto the porch after lunch, wielding a parasol to join her son and daughter on the beach where her son had placed two beach chairs beneath the green umbrella.

"Good grief, Mummy, you do look a fright!" Gloria exclaimed, catching sight of her as she made her way unsteadily over the sand dune.

"Please don't ridicule your poor old mother," Mrs. Murchison admonished as her son sprang to assist her to the beach chair beneath the umbrella.

"Mummy, when I tell people about you, they refuse to believe me!" an unrepentant Gloria continued. "You sound like Lady Bracknell, a miraculous survivor of Victorian melodrama!"

"Don't be ridiculous, my dear. Lady Bracknell was before my time."

"Come to think of it, Mummy, you do look remarkably like this photo of Edith Sitwell on the back cover of my Penguin." Gloria held up the paperback of Sitwell's *Poems* for her mother to see.

"Who's Edith Sitwell?" Ralph inquired, turning onto his back in the hot sand and peering up at his sister seated beside his mother.

"If you don't know who Edith Sitwell is, dear brother, I won't disabuse you," Gloria scolded in her mocking tone.

"Gloria, I thought you'd given up books and started to live?" Ralph said.

"If you both insist on thrusting this ignoble scheme upon me, I shall leave!" Gloria flared angrily. "I refuse to be pushed into anything, especially something that's been arranged. I've always insisted on leading my own life, and, dear Mother, I'm a woman of twenty-four, not a girl of sixteen. Besides, I've no wish whatever to be tied to some stupid male to become his drudging housewife and to raise a slew of brats. The very idea is appalling to me! I have chosen my career of independence, thank you!"

"Bravo, Gloria!" Ralph exclaimed when she'd finished her peroration. "But doancha see, you're off the hook, 'cause Mike took a fancy to Anne?"

"Off the hook?" Gloria repeated indignantly. "Brother, you're incredibly brutal about my feelings!"

"Come off it, Gloria, all I said wuz—"

"Ralph, if you really cared about your former dolly bird, you wouldn't have allowed Mother to drive you apart."

"Would you have your brother marry my housemaid?" Mrs. Murchison challenged, alarmed by the turn of the conversation.

"As far as Anne goes—" Ralph began to explain.

"Mother, Mrs. Proctor informed me that this incorrigible Yank got drunk last night at the Cockatoo Bar and into a punch-up with Anne's boyfriend, Tom Delaney, who has now taken his temptress back to Cairns," Gloria announced.

"Look, Gloria, Mum asked me to invite Mike ta come up 'ere for the Christmas hols," Ralph said. "I resisted at first but changed me mind, thinkin' that Mike could look after himself, for he'd decided to read in the Mitchell Library in Sinny."

"That would suit me just fine!" Gloria exclaimed, laughing. "In future I shall make my own holiday arrangements, for that is the best way not to be interfered with!"

"Maybe you've been saved from a worse fate?" Ralph coyly suggested.

"What do you mean?" Gloria asked, opening her eyes wide.

"Ya might 'ave fallen in love with a Maori?" Ralph teased, winking at his mother.

"Really, you are quite base!" Gloria cried, throwing a handful of sand in his face.

"Gloria!" Mrs. Murchison admonished.

"I know when I'm not wanted," Ralph said, pulling himself to his feet. "I'll give you a wide berth and stick to what I know best, caulkin' the *Sea Lark*."

As soon as her brother was out of earshot, Gloria said to her mother, "Ralph's perfectly right, of course. Mummy, your pretensions are what make us appear perfectly ridiculous in the eyes of the world."

"Don't talk nonsense, m'dear," Mrs. Murchison protested. "The invitation was your brother's. I believe I had nothing to do with it."

"Now who's talking nonsense, Mummy!" Gloria exclaimed, laughing. "You were in it up to your eyeballs!"

"Nowadays young people make their own social arrangement, but I find that they usually make a hash of them."

"You're really quite wonderful, aren't you, Mummy?" Gloria responded in her challenging manner. "In one breath you tacitly acknowledge your complicity and in the next you totally disown it. I do believe that you could teach me the art of lying till you're blue in the face!"

"When you've lived as long as I have, m'dear, you'll know how far the truth gets you," Mrs. Murchison said, unshaken.

"Well, Mummy, I simply refuse to be auctioned off to the highest bidder! If we don't have enough money to live on, why don't you sell some of the land? Ralph tells me that it is worth more than you paid for it, and it might be turned into building lots."

"I refuse to have the riffraff of Surface Paradise living at my doorstep!" Mrs. Murchison protested indignantly. "I'd rather be dead!"

"You could auction it off and live with me."

"What nonsense you talk!"

"Mummy, you can't live here in perfect isolation, no matter how baronial you might think it," Gloria chided. "You have no one to talk to from one year's end to the next. How many times must I urge you to come and live with me in Sydney?"

"Umph!" Mrs. Murchison protested. "I won't be beholden to my children."

Ralph called to them from atop the sand dune, "Mum! Gloria! Mike's headin' down the beach!"

"The wanton rooster approaches!" Gloria mockingly exclaimed. "Doubtless, Ralph is warning me not to offend his mate."

"The chicken has flown the coop, but now he's coming home again," Mrs. Murchison coyly observed.

"Mummy, you're perfectly incorrigible!" Gloria put her nose in her paperback.

Mrs. Murchison immediately addressed Michael when he'd reached them. "Have you had your lunch?"

"Thank you, Mrs. Murchison, but I'm not hungry," Michael responded evasively as he sat down on the sand beside Ralph, who was reading the *Brisbane Courier Mail*, while Gloria continued with Edith Sitwell's *Poems*, neither acknowledging his presence.

"Mike, an article 'ere says that Oral Roberts was arsed outta the country an' 'is itinerary was only 'arf finished," Ralph reported.

"What a perfectly dreadful experience for the poor man!" Mrs. Murchison said. "But he does have a strange name."

"Sounds like a brand of toothpaste ta me," Ralph said. "Mike an' I 'eard 'im address a footy match in Sinny. He turned up 'arftime an' mouthed a lot of codswallop 'bout what a wonderful game it was, but it wuz lousy."

"I guess that day he didn't save many souls?" Mrs. Murchison said, glancing at Gloria, who remained oblivious. "Michael, are you sure that you're not feeling peckish?"

"Thank you, Mrs. Murchison, but I'm not hungry," Michael repeated.

"I asked Mrs. Proctor to leave you a sandwich in the fridge," Mrs. Murchison noted. "It's her day to go to town, but I'm sure she's followed my instructions."

"Look, Mike, make Mum 'appy and go an' eat yer sandwich," Ralph urged his friend.

"All right, I will," Michael said, pulling himself to his feet and heading up over the sand dune to the house.

"Mum, why's Gloria actin' so bloody rude to Mike?" Ralph asked when Michael was out of earshot. "She totally ignored him!"

"Dear brother, I can live with your disapproval," Gloria remarked coolly. "Besides, I do find Edith Sitwell's *Poems* infinitely more interesting than your yobbo mate."

"My yobbo mate?" Ralph said, red-faced, as he appealed to his mother, "Wasn't Gloria rude to Mike?"

"You're attaching too much importance to a very slight matter," Gloria insisted. "Given the circumstances, I do believe that your friend is repugnant."

"How do you think I feel when my friend is insulted?" Ralph protested.

"Your remedy is to take your mate where he won't be offended by your sister?" Gloria suggested.

"Gloria's rude, ain't she, Mum?" Ralph said.

"These days one hardly expects civility from the young," Mrs. Murchison blandly said.

"I must say, Mummy, you're not being very helpful!" Gloria exclaimed, closing her book and getting up.

"If you're going back to the house, m'dear, make us some lemonade?" Mrs. Murchison asked.

"Me too; my throat's parched!" Ralph added.

"Humph!" Gloria snorted as she started up over the sand dune to the house.

In the mellow afternoon light, Gloria took six lemons from the net bag in the fridge and sliced them with a big kitchen knife on the drain board. The room was large and square, filled with sunlight, with cupboards on either side of the sink. In the center was a large square table and two windows looking toward the sea from above the sink.

"I didn't expect to upset you," Gloria heard a male voice behind her.

Quickly looking up, Gloria saw Michael in the doorway, wearing tan shorts and a T-shirt.

"Upset me?" Gloria asked, opening her dark eyes wide.

"Just now on the beach," Michael explained.

"I wasn't offended. Wasn't I reading?"

"You were reading, but you seemed offended."

"I can assure you that I wasn't in the least offended!"

"Well, I had the idea you were upset, as if I'd offended you."

"No, you hadn't in the least offended me," Gloria insisted. "I see that your sandwich is still awaiting you in the fridge."

"Yes, I've had lunch already," Michael said.

"At Mrs. Coleraine's, I expect—which concerns me not in the least!" Gloria replied, enjoying his embarrassment. "If you wish to make yourself useful, you might squeeze these lemons while I get the pitcher."

"Okay, sure," Michael replied, putting half a lemon in the juicer and squeezing it, while Gloria stretched for the pitcher on the top shelf. Stepping beside her, Michael took it down and placed it on the drain board.

"Thank you!" Gloria exclaimed. She rinsed the pitcher before setting it on the table so she could pour in the lemon juice. Meanwhile, Michael examined a glass bowl holding some dried vegetation above the sink, while Gloria put ice cubes in the pitcher.

"That's a terrarium," Gloria explained. "I gave Mrs. Proctor explicit instructions to care for it, but as you can see, she failed to water it, and it dried up."

"Where'd ya collect the plants?" Michael asked, turning as she placed four glasses on the tray beside the pitcher, which she filled with cold water.

"Last Christmas I got them from a billabong not far from here," Gloria said. "Would you like to help me make another?"

"Sure," Michael replied, looking into her dark-brown eyes as she thrust the tray with the pitcher and four glasses upon him.

Ralph saw his sister and Michael descending the sand dune and exclaimed, "Just in the nick! Me tongue's black!"

"Thank you, Michael—and Gloria!" Mrs. Murchison said, taking a glass of lemonade and immediately noting her daughter's changed attitude toward the young American. This was not merely because Gloria did not return to reading Edith Sitwell's *Poems* but because she sat down beside her mother under the umbrella with a thoughtful expression on her face.

About four o'clock, a high layer of stratus clouds crept across the sky, filtering the sun's intensity. Mrs. Murchison returned to the house and asked her son's assistance in crossing the sand dune. Ralph did not return to the beach but continued caulking the *Sea Lark*.

"If you don't watch out, you'll get sunburned!" Gloria remarked to the young American, who'd fallen asleep.

Sitting up, Michael blushed, seeing the others were gone. Standing, he brushed the sand from his long legs and put on the T-shirt, which he tucked into his shorts, and eyed Gloria suspiciously.

"You wouldn't be so tired, if you didn't stay out so late," Gloria said, suddenly catching herself up and surprised by her boldness.

Michael looked at her sheepishly.

"My brother tells me that you don't like young women with short hair."

"Your hair's short only because you choose to wear it that way."

"Do you think I'm searching for compliments?"

"No, I don't think that."

"How have you thought of me?"

"I've always thought you looked chic."

"Chic? Now you *will think* that I am fishing for compliments!" Gloria exclaimed. "We really must not talk about each other in this way—at least I mustn't! What precisely do you do at the American Legation?"

"I just shuffle papers about."

"Don't you have to meet certain educational qualifications?" Gloria inquired. "My brother makes his work sound terribly rote. Certainly you don't feel that way too?"

"As Ralph says, you could train monkeys to do our job in the visa section," Michael insisted.

"You won't mind, I trust, if I don't believe a word you're saying!" Gloria exclaimed, laughing.

"You see, I'm not makin' a career out of the State Department. It's a dead-end job, meant to keep me busy before I get on with my life."

"Are you being serious or merely attitudinalizing?"

"Believe me, Ralph and I are mere functionaries," Michael insisted. "We spend our days putting fine points on pencils and filling out long, tedious forms."

"Frankly, I don't believe you for a moment!" Gloria said.

Michael shrugged with a wry smile as they began climbing the sand dune, going back to the house.

After dinner Mrs. Murchison insisted on playing her favorite game, whist, and at ten o'clock Mrs. Proctor brought tea and toast. Mrs. Murchison then retired for the night with her Agatha Christie mystery as she winked at her son, urging him to withdraw as well.

"Oh, oreright!" Ralph exclaimed, smiling. "I know when I'm not wanted!"

Michael sat in the armchair beside the fireplace and lit an herbal cigarette, while Gloria drifted to the open window, where a gauzy curtain was blown into the room from off the sea like a ghostly skein. The only light came from the lamp beside the card table.

"I love Surface Paradise at night," Gloria said as she breathed in the air. "Can't you smell the salt from the sea?"

"Not smoking an herbal cigarette," Michael said as he blew the smoke above his head.

"Would you like to go for a stroll on the beach?" Gloria asked.

"Sure!"

Gloria left her shoes on the porch, and they walked barefooted over the sand dune to the sea's edge, where the moonlight was making a silvery pathway. For a while, they walked in silence over the hard wet sand by the shore.

"I've the distinct impression that everything you've told me about yourself has been meant to amuse, for you've told me nothing about yourself," Gloria said, looking in the moonlight at the side of his face.

"If I look at myself coldly, I'm a moralistic prig," Michael confessed. "But I hope that I'm not being that repulsive right now?"

"That should give me some idea of the kind of person you are?" Gloria said.

"Perhaps. I don't wish to bore you."

"Why do you act so superior?"

"When I first met Ralph, he thought me a cold, aloof bastard," Michael confessed.

"How could you be, if you couldn't see yourself?" Gloria asked. "Like most young men, I believe you're merely postulating."

They stopped and faced each other in the moonlight. Beneath her intellectual superiority, Gloria yearned for romance as much as a lady of medieval times. She yearned for the footsteps of her lover sounding in a hollowed, coffered room and stone passageways. She yearned to gaze at a joust from the turret of a castle. At such moments, in her mind's eye, she could imagine that she was surveying some delicately detailed landscape with green fields, gray villages, and a blunt Norman church spire with a castle beyond as if it were not a dream, but a reality.

"I've been very much alone," Michael confessed, "but it's best not to give way to self-pity."

Side by side they walked barefoot over the still-warm sand to the sand dune, where they sat between dry clumps of spinifex grass.

"When we lost Boonderoo, I lost my position as a grazier's daughter," Gloria explained. "It was a loss of social status, so I had to find a career of my own. In the normal course of events, I should have attended school dances, gone to Europe for a year, and upon graduation I should have married the boy from the neighboring sheep station, and so the cycle begins!"

"Do you miss Boonderoo?"

"Yes, it's an ache that won't go away," Gloria admitted. "It was a world that I thought would never end. My brother and I used to set off with our ponies and try to pass beyond the surrounding hills. Sometimes we followed a dry creek bed for an entire day, until we'd lost the creek bed underground. We descended into valleys over gray rocks covered with maidenhair fern. It was a landscape only the Aborigine could have seen before, belonging to the Dreamtime. But Boonderoo proved to be an illusion, so I've no desire to go back and see what's become of the place."

Gloria touched Michael's arms several times, as if to make sure of his attention, or to assure herself that she was not boring him.

"Has my brother told you that my mother had the idea of throwing us together?" Gloria suddenly asked him.

"Yeah, Ralph clued me in on that right away," Michael confessed. "I hope you don't feel offended?"

"Of course not. I'm not in the least offended," Gloria acknowledged frankly.

"Still, you might have felt a bit hurt?" Michael suggested. "But I'm glad you took it so lightheartedly."

"Have you ever dreamed of coming to a place like Surface Paradise?" Gloria asked.

"No, but maybe I've read about it in a book," Michael responded, standing and stretching. "I feel bushed!"

"Give me your hand?"

"Sure!"

For a moment they remained standing close together, her eyes sparkling in the moonlight.

"Do you know what time it is?" Gloria asked.

"It's eleven thirty," Michael said, freeing his hand to consult the luminous dial on his watch.

"Would you like to collect plants for my terrarium tomorrow?" Gloria asked.

"Yeah, I would."

"We won't have to go too far," Gloria said. "The billabong's in a dry creek bed not far from the Spit. I'll finish my article in the morning; then we can set off after lunch."

"Sure, maybe I'll make myself a terrarium," Michael said. "There's a good conversation piece, when you can't think of something to say."

"I shouldn't think you're ever at a loss for words!" Gloria said.

"You say that because you don't know me too well," Michael responded.

They strolled back to the house in the bright moonlight in silence by the edge of the sea. When they reached the house, Gloria said goodnight, and they abruptly parted. Michael climbed the stairs, brushing the rubbery tentacles of the plant on the landing. Quickly undressing, he lay on the bed naked in the moonlight, thinking that he must leave Surface Paradise first thing in the morning to go to Cairns to see Anne.

Awakened by a sharp rapping, Michael opened his eyes, reached for his watch on the wooden chair beside the bed, and saw that it was eight o'clock.

"'Ave you forgotten yer promise ta help me caulk the *Sea Lark* this mornin'?" Ralph asked, entering the bedroom and slumping into the wooden chair before the open window, his legs stretched out before him.

"I'm sorry, Ralph, but I can't—not today," Michael insisted, putting on a fresh pair of underpants, pulling up his cord pants, then putting on his surfer's sport shirt. Sitting down on the bed, he put on his socks, then thrust his feet into his scuffed white bucks.

"I 'ope yer not goin' ta make a fool of yerself 'bout Anne?" Ralph asked suspiciously, eyeing his friend.

"Willya mind yer own business, Ralph!" Michael protested.

"Look, mate, doan' get stroppy wi' me," Ralph replied, pulling himself to his feet.

"I'm sorry, Ralph, but I have thought this through, and I know exactly what I'm doin' now," Michael explained. "I've decided to leave Surface Paradise this morning, and I'd really appreciate it if you'd speak with your mother and thank her for her hospitality. But the fact of the matter is that, given the circumstances, I just couldn't face her."

"Ya know, my mum will be offended if ya do a bunk," Ralph retorted, taken aback.

"Believe me, Ralph, I couldn't face her. So put my abrupt departure in the best possible light and tell your sister the same thing, willya?" Michael pleaded.

"Leave my sister outta this, or I'll knock yer block off, ya conceited bastard!" Ralph angrily exclaimed.

"Okay, I'll speak to your mother myself and explain—which is what I should have done in the first place."

When Michael and Ralph reached the dining room, they found Mrs. Murchison and her daughter having breakfast. Mrs. Murchison looked formidable at the head of the board, while Gloria, in a lime-green cotton blouse and white pants, gave them a cheery, "Good morning!" With this, she immediately explained to her mother, "Michael and I are going to collect plants for my new terrarium this afternoon, but unfortunately this morning I must finish my article, for I have a deadline facing me, and it must be posted by Friday."

"Gloria, seein' that ya will be busy this mornin', Mike can 'elp me caulk the *Sea Lark*," Ralph said, as they sat down to grapefruit.

"What's your article about, Gloria?" Michael asked, ignoring Ralph, but wincing when the grapefruit burned his split lip.

"The latest bathing suit fashions," Gloria said.

"Male or female?" Ralph asked, winking at Michael.

"Don't be silly, female of course!" Gloria exclaimed.

"Nowadays the bathing costumes of both sexes are perfectly ridiculous," Mrs. Murchison allowed, putting on a face.

"Ta please me, all the sheila 'as ta do is ta swim in the buff," Ralph ventured, grinning.

"That, I'm sure, would please you immensely, dear brother!" Gloria exclaimed, laughing.

That morning, as good as his word, Michael dutifully helped Ralph caulk the *Sea Lark*, but after lunch he set off with Gloria down a red-earth road into the intense heat. Having changed into tan shorts and a brown twill shirt, Michael still wore his white bucks. In one hand he carried a galvanized bucket containing wetted burlap to keep the plant specimens alive; in the other he held a short-handled spade. Gloria wore green denim slacks and a long-sleeved blouse of the same material.

Overhead the stringy-bark was smothered by great vines that blocked out the sunlight, while unseen birds screeched from the green canopy above. The couple's faces were glowing with perspiration from the oppressive heat. Reaching an iron bridge, they looked down through chains of vines into the billabong, which was directly below. A white heron stood on stilt-like legs in the brackish water, its small head turned to them, looking with one eye. Even while they watched, they felt that they were intruders, for the white heron raised its wings and flapped above them, moving slowly among the branches toward the blue sky.

"That's our billabong," Gloria announced.

They began a steep descent to the muddy creek, Michael going first to push the vines aside. At the bottom grew a bush with dark, shiny green leaves and small white flowers.

"That's a peppercorn bush," Gloria explained.

"Is that where pepper comes from?"

"Yes, haven't you seen one before?"

"No, I haven't."

Sitting beside the billabong, Michael removed his shoes and socks and stepped into the tepid water, his feet sinking into the mud. Carefully he dug some moss and a small fern, then wrapped them in wet burlap and placed them in the bucket. Finding a particularly good specimen, he smiled at Gloria, a boyish smile, and wiped his brow, leaving a reddish muddy streak across his face.

Most men protest that you're never out of their mind, Gloria thought as she worked beside Michael. *But I needn't fear that in his case!* "There's another billabong just farther along," Gloria pointed out.

Beyond some dense vegetation, they saw a blue column of smoke that rose straight into the air before them.

"It's a sundowner!" Gloria whispered behind him. "Let's go back!"

But Gloria's words had alerted the sundowner, for he stood up and greeted them.

"Hello!" Michael said to him.

"Hello yerself!" the sundowner replied with seeming indifference. Maybe he didn't see many people, though his eyes were bright and friendly, but his gray stubble made him look like a hobo. He was wearing olive-drab trousers that looked to be of military issue, with suspenders and a gray shirt of the same olive-drab material, the sleeves coming down to his wrists. His wide-brimmed hat had corks hanging from the brim to ward off mozzies, and on his feet he wore a pair of stout boots. His personal effects, his swag, might have been placed in his ground blanket, along with his cooking utensils and another pair of boots. His billy hung over the fire on a short length of wood, held by a forked stick.

"Where ya headed?" Michael asked the sundowner, squatting opposite him across the fire.

"Tassie, if I git that fer," the sundowner said.

"Have you ever thought of settlin' down, maybe getting' married?" Michael asked slyly.

"I couldn't take havin' four walls 'bout me fer long," the sundowner confessed. "Onc't I spent some time in Sinny, which I couldn't abide, so I left."

"Whaddya do fer a livin'?"

"Off season I repair shears, whedder 'lectric or fuel-powered makes no dif'rence ta me," the sundowner boasted. "Havin' a skill, I can always find work."

Gloria remembered swagmen coming to Boonderoo to work the sheepshearing, then leave the bunkhouse early one morning, going off as mysteriously as the Abos, who felt the urge to go walkabout. Such men resented all family ties, or had long ago forgotten them.

Michael spoke in low tones to the sundowner, interspersed with the easy laughter of men who are adept at getting into contact with the primal male consciousness that renounces all claims of family and society. The male ego is often too painful to think about.

Better to be in touch with the primal male consciousness, to wipe civilization off the slate, to obliterate everything. Or simply to await a new consciousness, come as it must, giving them a new perspective as the pendulum swings back and forth.

Why does Michael give the sundowner such rapt attention? Gloria asked herself, feeling excluded. *Is that what Michael wants, to wander forever, to be the detached male? Am I unprepared to accept this new country?*

Suddenly Gloria felt tied to a man's heels, feeling only a sense of revulsion, although she felt herself on the verge of a new experience, preparing to make the most important commitment she'd ever made in her life, yet feeling unprepared to make it, to submit to the male ego. She felt only the urge to go back to be what once she had been, to wipe the slate clean, obliterate everything, awaiting a new perspective that must somehow come. But already the lightness of his restless body was in her arms, his heart pressed against hers, already the leap she knew she would make had landed her she knew not where, as if the slender baby were already in her arms, and she would press it against her heart, for she had entered a savage country, putting aside her clothes, for they would live like animals without their skin.

Gloria gazed down at the arch of his back. How beautiful he was. In her pride she had been unbroken but was suddenly shattered, for her wandering spirit had burst forth. She knew that she would not forget him, but would become a part of him, like the roots that absorb the rain.

After bidding the sundowner good-bye, they made their way back along the dry creek bed to the iron bridge, where they sat on a slanting gray rock and put on their socks and shoes. With the collected plants, they climbed the steep path to the iron bridge and started down the red-earth road in the direction of the Spit, where blood-red orchids clung to the trunks of the stringy barks. Michael broke off a sprig and thrust it in Gloria's hair above her ear.

When they reached the Spit, they climbed to the top and sat in a hollow between clumps of spinifex grass. In the blue sky, seagulls circled, their long cries coming from the top of the sky. Below they saw the quiet lagoon enclosed by a coral reef, where a white froth of foam marked the narrow entrance of the channel, beyond which lay the South Pacific Ocean.

"What do you want from your life?" Gloria asked him.

"Lately I've thought of leaving the American Legation and going to a German university to learn the language properly and absorb German culture," Michael said. "My father's idea was that I follow him into stockbroking, but that doesn't appeal to me."

"Why did you end up in the State Department?" Gloria asked, looking into his eyes.

"My perversity, I guess!" Michael confessed, laughing.

"I like people who have definite goals and the resolution to carry them out," Gloria averred. "What would you do with your education?"

"Nothing really. I don't have any definite goals—just personal culture," Michael insisted. "Am I being selfish?"

"No, but you can't live on your ego," Gloria replied. "You must have some idea of what you would do with your learning?"

"I should be satisfied to spend my whole life gathering together the wisdom to write one book," Michael confessed. "A golden book, it would be filled with important insights, like Marcus Aurelius's *Meditations*. It would be read for the pleasure of reading it, giving the reader insights into my experience, like Thoreau's *Walden*, an invitation to solitude and contemplation."

Kneeling before her, Michael shaped his thoughts with his hands, invoking them with the perfect insight of inspiration. "Maybe I just sound foolish!"

"No, not in the least," Gloria insisted, smiling. "I feel elevated by what you say, but ask myself, is it only an escape?"

"Or my being selfish?"

"But some things are worth fighting for," Gloria protested. "I don't belittle your aspirations, for I admire your commitment. Perhaps I fear that it requires a great deal of determination, the task you propose."

Late that afternoon they walked back along the red-earth road to the house, neither saying much. Michael picked another blood-red orchid and, placing it in her hair behind her left ear, said, "Perhaps this one won't fall out!"

"Is my hair cut too short?" Gloria asked him, smiling.

"No, I like your hair, and it isn't cut too short," Michael insisted.

"You liar!" Gloria exclaimed, laughing.

At dinner that evening Ralph reported that he'd been to Surface Paradise and bought sails for the *Sea Lark*, not to mention his outlay for paint.

"Tomorrow mornin', mate, ya'll be helpin' me ta paint," Ralph advised Michael.

"Tomorrow Michael and I have plans to drive to Boonderoo," Gloria said, looking very chic in her beige linen pantsuit and cream-colored silk blouse.

"Whatcha goin' dare fer?" Ralph asked, dumbstruck.

"To be perfectly frank, Michael has summoned up my courage," Gloria said. "But I believe that I shall shed tears over all the wasted human effort we expended at Boonderoo."

"The station, I understand, is now roofless and being used as a sheepfold," Mrs. Murchison remarked sadly. "I for one will never go there again, having no desire to go back on my life, you see?"

"Gloria, what 'bout the article you're supposed to write?" Ralph asked.

"I shall simply postpone mailing it for a day or two."

After dinner Mrs. Murchison insisted on her nightly game of whist, Michael being paired with Gloria and she with her son. Although Gloria was as good a player as her mother, that night she was distracted and restless, filled with a suppressed excitement that showed on her face. Her mother knew that it was the young

American who'd brought about this sudden transformation in her daughter, for although Mrs. Murchison had never fallen in love, she was wise enough to know that a sudden revolution had taken place in her daughter's heart, and dramatic changes appealed to her sense of the theatrical. She was delighted that her daughter had found love instead of revulsion. If Mrs. Murchison had one theory about the proper relations of the sexes, it consisted in her belief that a young woman not insist too much on her own blessed individuality, but find her happiness in making some young man believe that she is indispensable to his happiness, especially when the young man has money.

After dinner they retired to the living room, where Gloria tripped lightly to the liquor cabinet and began juggling bottles with a painter's eye for pretty colors.

"Isn't it too late for a drink, Gloria?" Mrs. Murchison asked. "In this hot weather won't alcohol heat the blood?"

"The night's a kitten, Mummy!" Gloria protested. "Wouldn't you like crème de menthe? Or are you going to insist on your tea and toast, with beddy-byes at ten?" Holding up a green liqueur, Gloria peered into the curved bottle.

"All right, I'll have a crème de menthe—not wishing to be a killjoy with my own daughter."

"Mummy pretends not to like a liqueur, but she often has a bit in the evening," Gloria noted. "Why not, when they have such pretty names and lovely colors?"

"What's got into you tonight, Gloria?" Ralph asked, disgusted. "I never 'eard you talk such abysmal rot!"

"Forgive me, dear brother," Gloria responded, crossing the living room to give her mother her crème de menthe. "But Mummy and I have every right to get whatever pleasure we can out of life."

"Please don't speak for me!" Mrs. Murchison protested with theatrical exaggeration. "You make me feel quite uncomfortable."

"Why be dull and conventional, Mummy?" Gloria challenged her. "Why don't you live life to the full? What do you think would happen if I were to mix all these pretty colors? Michael, will you please be my guinea pig?"

"I've drunk a lot of rotgut in my time!" Michael exclaimed, laughing, but looking ill at ease as he sprawled in the armchair beside the fireplace.

"Make him a quadruple-lord," Mrs. Murchison suggested.

"What's that, Mummy?" Gloria inquired.

"Put a jigger of chartreuse and a jigger of Benedictine into a tall glass," Mrs. Murchison said. "Then add some rum. You'll find the Bundaberg rum on the bottom shelf. Then fill the glass with orange juice."

"That sounds like a zombie!" Michael exclaimed.

"Okay, Gloria, make me one too," Ralph relented. "I'll get some orange juice from the fridge."

At that moment Mrs. Proctor appeared, asking if she should bring tea and toast.

"Heavens, no!" Mrs. Murchison exclaimed, laughing.

"Don't you think we're being rather dull and conventional?" Gloria asked Michael, having given him his quadruple-lord and sitting on the love seat beside her mother. "Besides, what's wrong with our getting squiffy? We must learn to throw caution to the wind! I do believe that this old house would make a perfect location for an assignation, with dear Mother as the perfect madam!"

"Gloria, shame on you!" Mrs. Murchison exclaimed.

"You do talk such rot!" Ralph cried to his sister.

"If I've offended you, dear brother, it's because what's sauce for the goose is sauce for the gander," Gloria said. "You and Michael evidently believe that it's perfectly all right that you should do whatever you please, just so long as it doesn't come home. Isn't that male hypocrisy?"

"I don't wish to provoke a fight between brother and sister," Michael said lamely as he threw back his quadruple-lord, the hot liquor burning down his throat.

"Oh, but my brother and I love to fight!" Gloria said to them.

Ralph had never seen his sister look more beautiful, her whole body radiating heat and energy. *If not of alcohol, then of what?* Ralph asked himself, but he'd seen it all quite clearly, saying to himself, *Gloria will let nothin' stand in her way, and the poor sod's too bemused and clueless to see it!*

"Well, it's past my bedtime!" Mrs. Murchison announced, standing. "I bid you both good night—and Ralph, I've a particular word to say to you."

"G'night," Ralph said sheepishly, taking his mother's meaning.

After they'd left, Michael sat in the armchair beside the fireplace, with Gloria standing, looking strikingly beautiful in the soft moonlight from above the sea, for she'd switched off the lamp on the card table. The white gauzy curtains billowed in, propelled by a breeze from off the sea. Michael had lit an herbal cigarette and was listening to the waves breaking on the shore, the only sound.

"Would you like to stroll along the beach?" Gloria asked.

"Sure!" Michael replied, glad that their words had broken the silence that enveloped them.

They left their shoes on the porch and walked over the sand dune in the iridescent moonlight, heading in a southerly direction along the shore. Michael thought of a call he'd made that afternoon to Anne, using the phone in the hall.

"Who'd ya say ya wanted to speak to?"

"Anne!"

"She ain't 'ere!" and the phone had been slammed down.

Walking beside Gloria in the moonlight, Michael hadn't been able to put Anne out of his thoughts, for he'd been arguing with himself, saying that he might have won her if things had been different, but everything had worked so fast, and he'd been asking himself if he'd been crushed by Fate, his worst fears realized, before he knew where he was.

"I was thinking of our little understanding," Gloria announced, breaking the silence.

"What understanding?" Michael asked.

"You know, my mother's throwing us together. Then you said to me last night that I shouldn't be offended because it hadn't worked."

"I don't think your mother meant any harm," Michael replied, feeling like a ninny.

"You're just like my brother—an expert in deflating the ego!" Gloria exclaimed.

"Perhaps Ralph got the knack from me, but—"

"Please don't apologize!"

Michael was thinking how warm Anne was. *But what's wrong with being ambitious and intellectual?* he thought.

The moonlight rose higher above the sea, losing its dusky redness. Gloria's face looked wide awake, expectant, as she focused all her attention upon him. He couldn't bear the bold virginity shining in her face.

They climbed the sand dune and sat in the still-warm hollow between clumps of spinifex grass. Michael put his arms about her shoulders, then gently squeezed her arm. She put her arm about his waist, holding his hip. He turned to her and kissed her neck, then her lips. She encircled his neck, and he kissed her lips again, her breath coming in hot snatches. A burning fire seemed to consume them, burning within, as she moved her hands over his body. They lay back in the warm sand, holding each other and kissing. He felt that she would devour him, like the female praying mantis devours its mate after fecundation.

Suddenly she pushed him away and stood up, looking at the moon above the sea. "You hate me!"

"No, I don't hate you," Michael protested.

"You hate me for being myself!"

He touched her arm gently until she turned to him, and he held her in his arms. She sobbed at her sudden switching, terrible sensuality, for it had been a mistake. But she couldn't help feeling vulnerable. She was a cool marble goddess on a pedestal, meant to be admired, but having no idea that, since she'd fallen in love, she must be toppled.

"You love Anne Coleraine—you must go to her!" Gloria admonished.

"No, I love you," Michael protested, not thinking that he was lying, for he'd always loved in more directions than his heart would account for. "Besides, Anne's gone back to Cairns to be with Tom Delaney."

"Shouldn't you forget her, then?" Gloria asked.

"Yeah," Michael ruefully confessed, not wishing to be unfaithful to Anne, who'd rejected him.

They walked back to the house on the packed wet sand by the shore and climbed the sand dune in front of the house. They picked up their shoes from the porch and went into the living room, where Gloria lit the lamp upon the table.

"Michael, I love you," she whispered, turning to him from the card table.

"I love you too," Michael responded, holding her in his arms as he kissed her lips.

After Gloria put out the light, they climbed the stairs and parted where the rubbery-branched plant stood as a sentinel.

Michael saw a light shining from beneath his door. Ralph was sprawled in the straight-backed wooden chair before the open window, his legs thrust out in front of him.

"Mike, I doan' wancha leadin' me sister down the primrose path," Ralph immediately announced, pulling himself slowly to his feet.

"I doan' know whatcher talkin' 'bout," Michael protested.

"Ain't ya supposed to be bonkers 'bout Anne?"

"Why doancha mind yer own business!"

"Doan' get stroppy wi' me, mate!"

"Believe me, Ralph, I know what I'm doin'," Michael insisted, his tone softening.

"Doan' take my sister ta Boonderoo tomorra," Ralph urged.

"Gloria's made up her own mind."

"Like the cat that got the cream, is that it?" Ralph taunted him. "Ya conceited bastard!"

"Frig off!" Michael exclaimed angrily as Ralph stormed out.

Alone, Michael quickly undressed and lay on his back naked on the bed in the moonlight. He didn't wish to lose Ralph as a good friend, but then he didn't wish to disappoint Gloria—any more than he wished to lose Anne. Drawing a deep breath, he felt too tired to think; ever since he'd arrived at Surface Paradise, he'd found thinking harder and harder.

Maybe I should cut out first thing in the morning and go straight up to Cairns and be with Anne and say nothing to anybody? Michael thought, but he felt he'd been hit on the head with a mallet, and soon he was in the arms of Morpheus.

17

The following morning Michael was awakened by a sharp rapping on the door. “Gi’ me a moment!” he exclaimed, springing to his feet and pulling on his cord slacks, not bothering with the underpants, and opening the door to find Gloria wearing khaki slacks, a twill blouse, and gum-soled shoes.

“You do look a pretty sight!” Gloria cried. “Don’t you know it’s seven?”

“I’m sorry. I musta forgot we’re goin’ to Boonderoo!”

“Please be slippy, will you?” Gloria admonished. “Mrs. Proctor is getting our breakfast.”

After shaving quickly, Michael pulled on his surfer’s sports shirt. Then he sat on the bed to put on his socks and scuffed white bucks. Gloria was in the dining room, holding up breakfast.

“Mrs. Proctor has prepared an English breakfast,” Gloria explained. “She has also done us a luncheon hamper to take along.”

“I’m in good hands, I see!” Michael exclaimed with a wry smile.

After breakfast they went outside, where already the heat was intense, and they crossed the rough burned grass to the doorless garage, smothered beneath a hardenbergia vine. In the dimly lit interior stood the antiquated Singer Roadster that Colonel Murchison had imported from England before the war.

“Can you drive on the left-hand side of the road?” Gloria asked as she handed him the key.

"Sure!" Michael insisted, frowning as he stepped to the driver's seat, after opening the door for her.

"Ralph filled the petrol tank yesterday," Gloria explained.

Michael searched for the ignition switch in the dim light.

"There it is!" Gloria explained, holding his hand to guide him.

"Thanks," Michael muttered as he put the key in the ignition and ground the engine, once, twice, then again.

"Please don't drain the battery!" Gloria advised. "Talk to her gently. Daddy always called her Nelly."

"After King Charles's mistress?" Michael asked, turning to meet her eyes in the dim light.

"Yes, you must coax her," Gloria explained.

"Okay, I'll coax her!" Michael replied, hunching over and turning the key. After a few moments, the engine sputtered, then died.

"But you didn't coax her!" Gloria protested.

"What the devil am I supposed to say?!"

"Please don't be pigheaded. Here, let me try!"

"Sure!" Michael exclaimed, pushing the driver's door open and stepping out, while Gloria slipped behind the wheel.

"Really, Nelly, Michael didn't mean to treat you unkindly," Gloria coaxed, turning the key in the ignition. Slowly the engine hiccupped, vibrated, and started uncertainly.

Michael had stepped around the vehicle and now sat in the passenger's seat.

"You're the man—you must drive," Gloria advised.

"Nelly's very stubborn, I see," Michael commented as he headed back to the driver's seat.

"Do you mean that I'm very stubborn too?" Gloria challenged, when he was seated behind the wheel.

"Aren't you?" Michael replied, meeting her eyes, a grin on his face.

All morning they drove across a brown, sunburned landscape where the gum trees lifted their white arms toward the eternal blue sky, with their long, slim, pale-green leaves hardly casting a shadow on the bright earth. The hot air hit the windshield, propelling insects to strike it with their hard bodies. Beyond Goondiwindi they turned off the unsealed road and stopped shortly afterward, where Gloria pointed out the first boundary stone that marked the beginning of Boonderoo Station.

Getting out, they looked down into a dry valley that seemed to belong to the moon, save the heated air that rose from below, shimmering, distorting the earth, making it look insubstantial, like a mirage. After a moment they could hear the far-off bleating of sheep.

"The station house is over there," Gloria indicated, pointing.

"Are you sure that you wish to see this old place again?" Michael asked, seeing the tears in her eyes.

"It seems that nothing is left that I remember," Gloria remarked, choking up.

"Come, you must face it!" Michael urged.

"Yes, I suppose I must," Gloria conceded, turning to get the wicker hamper out of the backseat and handing it to him. "It's too hot to eat here. Let's have our picnic in the shade of the station house."

Descending the hillside, they heard myriad insects in the burned grass, mingling with the bleating of the sheep. When they'd reached the roofless station house, Michael stepped through the aperture that had once been the front door and noted dried sheep's dung.

"Daddy's office was over here," Gloria explained, standing on the spot, while Michael set down the hamper beside the wall. "This is where he conducted station business, listened to the wireless, or read."

"What books did he have?" Michael asked.

"He didn't have many. He was very fond of Dickens and had a complete set of his novels, along with 'Banjo' Paterson's poems and the King James Bible, which he would read to us aloud." Stepping through a hole in the back wall, Gloria continued, "Mummy's kitchen garden was right here, where she grew her English gooseberries and red currants for jam and jelly, not to mention her favorite English flowers. She'd water them furiously every year, but the fierce sun always burned them up."

"Why didn't your mother grow native plants?" Michael asked, noting how exquisite Gloria's oval face was, for she looked like her mother.

"Mummy wished to have a little piece of England in the red dust of Australia—but she failed," Gloria lamented. "Just as she failed to make Ralph and me proper English children."

"Maybe she failed with your brother, but she didn't fail to make an English lady of you," Michael retorted, laughing.

"Well, she certainly did try!"

Gloria unpacked the hamper, producing a bottle of Australian wine and two plastic glasses. "This chablis is from the Barossa Valley," she said and handed him a glass filled to the brim.

"And here I thought it was your famous Queensland pineapple wine your brother once tol' me about," Michael said before taking a sip.

"I can assure you that my brother was pulling your leg," Gloria replied.

"Tastes good, anyway." Michael took another sip.

"In Queensland I suppose everything's got something to do with pineapple," Gloria conceded, smiling at him.

"So why not pineapple wine, huh?"

"Seeing you fancy everything Australian, I'll have Mrs. Proctor make you a bug sandwich," Gloria suggested, giving him a sandwich from the hamper.

"Not being an Abo, I'm not particularly fond of bugs!" Michael said, eyeing the sandwich suspiciously. "Besides, bugs are too ugly to eat."

"So is a lobster, come to think of it. Try it!"

"Tastes good, anyway," Michael took a big bite.

"Michael, please don't devour your sandwich in two bites!"

"Sorry. D'ya like livin' in Paddo?"

"Yes, but I shan't stay there forever," Gloria said, looking off into the blue distance. "After all, you've seen my dog kennel in Paddington! When I was a child, I loved the freedom of Boonderoo, the sense of having so much land about me. I suppose it is freedom I want most. That's why I envy you your independence, for you can come and go just as you please, unfettered by petty human emotions."

For Michael it was as if Anne Coleraine was speaking, using the same words as Gloria, for hadn't she charged him with being dispassionate, an egoist, uninvolved in the lives of others?

"Do you remember my brother bringing you 'round to my flat last January?" Gloria asked. "It was a frightfully hot day, and after lunch we went swimming at Bondi Beach?"

"Yeah, I remember sitting on your wrought-iron balcony with its bird's-eye view of the Sydney Cricket Grounds."

"I've a snapshot of you both that I took that day," Gloria said as if possessed by memory. "You both looked so happy that I captioned it in my scrapbook 'Two Mates Together.'"

"Yeah, I hadn't been long in Australia then," Michael said.

"Money makes a big difference in the way we lead our lives, don't you think?" Gloria asked, thinking of him again.

"What would you do if you had a lot of money?"

"I'd buy a house in the suburbs with lots of land about it, where I'd make a home for my mother."

"Makes sense."

"I don't expect you to understand."

"I do. Really I do."

It was eight o'clock when they returned to Surface Paradise, where Gloria's mother had postponed dinner for them. Afterward, Mrs. Murchison insisted on her nightly game of whist. At ten o'clock Mrs. Proctor appeared with tea and toast, and Mrs. Murchison retired with a new Agatha Christie mystery. Ralph had eyed his sister suspiciously all evening, thinking that she'd changed into a white brocade dress for no good purpose. He watched as she stepped lightly from the card table to the open window, saying she wished to breathe in the fresh air. Her dark hair she'd swept up at the back of her head and secured with a tortoiseshell comb. It was her radiance and her restlessness that made Ralph feel that he was the unwanted third person.

"Mike, would ya like ta help me paint the *Sea Lark* tomorra mornin'?" Ralph asked, sitting up.

"Sure," Michael replied as he stood beside the fireplace, smoking an herbal cigarette.

After her brother had left the living room, Gloria asked, "Michael, would you like to go for a stroll on the beach?"

"Sure, I'd like to very much," he replied, wondering as much as Ralph about her restlessness.

On the porch Gloria paused, placing her hand on his shoulder as she stooped to slip off her shoes. Then Michael sat on the step and took off his shoes and socks, leaving them on the porch. They climbed the sand dune before the house in the moonlight and walked down to the hard, wet sand by the shore. The waves had cast white spume on the beach that looked like the work of some mad washerwoman.

As they walked, he put his arm about her waist, and when she stopped and turned to him, he could see the bright moonlight shining in her eyes. They kissed and continued walking until they'd reached the Spit, which loomed palely above them. They climbed halfway to the top and sat in the still-warm sand.

"I'll leave my door unlocked tonight," Gloria said matter-of-factly as she slipped her hand beneath his shirt above his heart.

"Yes," Michael breathed, feeling strangely remote, almost as if someone else were speaking.

It was midnight when they returned to the house. Gloria said good-bye in the ordinary way, acting as if she hadn't expected him to kiss her. From his bedroom window Michael stared blankly at the waves breaking against the white shore. Lying on his back on the bed, he smoked an herbal cigarette, grateful to inflate his lungs. It seemed to him that he was falling back into the unimaginable past of the Australian continent, the stony silence of the dead heart, where no white man has set foot and maybe no Aborigine either—falling back into the darkness of an abyss.

Is it time I left Australia? he asked himself.

He remembered the little steamer of Lake Geneva that blew its whistle each time it arrived at a different town, and the three-piece Alsatian band playing sentimental German tunes. Again he was in Paris, inhaling the fragrance of the woman's perfume in the dark bedroom, her silvery limbs pale in the moonlight.

After opening his door silently, Michael slipped to the landing, brushing past the rubbery plant whose grotesque tentacles reached out to him from the glazed pot. When he reached Gloria's door, he turned the doorknob slowly. She was standing beside the bed in a pink dressing gown, with a look of surprise on her face. He closed the door behind him, sliding the bolt and leaning against it. His eyes ran to the other door that might lead to her mother's bedroom, which he also bolted.

"Mummy sleeps like a log," Gloria whispered, confirming his suspicion, as she removed her dressing gown, revealing her nightdress, her breasts visible beneath the sheer material. With a radiant smile she pushed the nightdress off her shoulders as Michael's eyes ran from the gentle swell of her stomach to the fullness of her breasts. Undressing quickly, he lifted her in his arms and laid her gently on the bed.

His breath came quickly as he took her in his arms, so that soon they were hollow-boned birds that rise above the earth as they embrace. A night of passion. But toward morning, the force of passion had lifted them up, dropping them into the depths of the sea.

Michael opened his eyes with a start and grabbed his watch from the wooden chair beside the bed. *Eleven!* Then he remembered coming back to his room at dawn, after spending a passionate night with Gloria. But now he felt as if it hadn't happened, so that he chastised himself, and deep in his heart, despite all the evidence to the contrary, he had the puritanical belief that if you slept with a girl, you should marry her.

If only Gloria hadn't put me on my mettle, Michael reasoned with himself, *by offering herself so blatantly. Maybe I did take advantage of her—maybe I didn't?—but that is now a moot point, because I feel such a deep tenderness for her and so admire her sophistication, for she always says the right thing at the right time and always feels right about herself, with a positive, morally uplifting attitude. In a perfect world, nothing could come between us. So why don't I love her?* Michael again asked himself as he stared blankly at the ceiling. *Hey, it's never easy when a girl takes advantage of a guy! That's the irony of fate, if you will.*

Michael sprang naked from the bed and gazed out the window into the bright sunlight. Ralph had managed to pull the *Sea Lark* about to the front of the house and was busy putting on a coat of spanking-new white paint. Someone he couldn't make out was wielding a paintbrush, but her torso was concealed by the sail, which Ralph had raised in the hot still air, so that all he could make out was her beautiful legs, which emphatically assured him of her sex.

"Hi! I'll be right down!" Michael called, kneeling at the window so as not to be seen.

Anne popped out from beneath the sail, wearing a pale-green bathing cozzie—the same she'd worn the first time he'd seen her.

"Hi!" Anne said.

Quickly putting on his khaki shorts and surfer's sports shirt, Michael thrust his feet into his sandals before clattering downstairs and out into the hot sunlight. Ralph was just painting "Sea Lark" in bright-red paint on the stern.

"She looks as if she's ready to take out," Michael said to Ralph while looking at Anne, who'd jumped from the sailboat and was standing beside Ralph, her paintbrush in her hand.

"Anne, when d'ya get back?" Michael asked.

"Las' night," she tersely replied.

"Weren't ya supposed ta stay for two weeks?"

"I didn't."

"I wanna talk to ya."

"We doan' have anything to talk about," Anne replied coolly as she turned to Ralph, who finished painting the *Sea Lark.*

"I'm glad ya've come back, Anne—but I guess you'd have been happier if I'd slugged your boyfriend?" Michael said.

"I'm sorry about that *too*," Anne replied.

Why's Anne standing beside Ralph, just as if she were still his girlfriend? Michael asked himself. *The poor bastard's probably never stopped loving her, and now he's ready to make his pitch again! So much for friendship between mates when a sheila gets involved! Or does Anne think me unmanly because I didn't slug that brute boyfriend of hers?*

Michael was breathing quickly, shallowly.

"Anne, can we go to Coo-ee?" he asked, using the name her mother had called her bungalow.

"Mummy's gone shoppin'," Anne said with an air of finality, looking to Ralph as if for moral support.

"We ain't finished paintin', mate," Ralph said, adopting the male version of Anne's tone.

Sitting in the hot sand, Michael watched them paint. After a while Ralph said good-bye to Anne, pointedly ignoring his friend, and returned to the house. Anne climbed the sand dune and walked down the beach to the shoreline, with Michael trailing after her. He knew that he'd made a mistake and wanted to confess, but all that he felt was a lump in his throat.

When they'd reached the overturned lifeboat, Anne turned to him, and he could see the pain in her eyes—or was it pity?—for he suspected that she was still in love with Ralph, which only made things more difficult. At that moment he felt the most intense need of her, a need that was brought into focus by the night he'd just spent with Gloria. He'd taken the wrong turn—that was all—gone right over the precipice. Somehow he must muster the courage to turn back and retrace his steps. A helpless futility and confusion had taken possession of him. All that he knew in the clear light of morning was that he'd made a dramatic mistake, and he wanted to confess to her that he'd acted basely, but he hesitated in doing so, fearing her reaction.

When they'd reached the bungalow, Michael followed Anne into the parlor, and she immediately rattled through the beaded curtain, and he followed her to her bedroom down the hall.

"Michael, I'm going to change!" Anne exclaimed, turning to him.

"Jeez, I'm sorry!" Michael said. He slipped back to the parlor and sat on the sofa, his elbows on his knees, the palms of his hands pressed into his eye sockets. Sitting up, he leaned back against the rose-pink cushion, his eyes falling on the gimcrackery surroundings. In the middle of the room on the round table was a seashell ashtray with "Surface Paradise" written in red script. The bamboo-framed pictures of rosy-cheeked nymphs and swains greeted him like old friends. The only addition to the decorating was a bell jar on the circular table, inside which a golden songbird was perched on a twig. Feeling a deep sense of contentment with this trumpery, Michael felt that it was the portent of a world he'd never known, but always yearned for, for he thought that he'd be happy to live there with Anne forever.

Awaiting Anne's return, Michael rested his head on a pink rose cushion, with his legs drawn up.

After closing the bedroom door, Anne stood before the narrow full-length mirror attached to the front of the closet door. Slowly she unpeeled her pale-green, one-piece bathing suit, cupping her breasts and squeezing them, imagining it was Michael holding them. The warmth of the sun had suffused her body. Now she knew that the appeal of Tom Delaney had been founded on her own vain emotions, for she'd taken pleasure in being seen with him as he represented strong male protection. Even though Tom accepted her without question, when they were alone together, she was terribly bored by his dullness, realizing that his professions of love were of a similar nature.

Then she thought of Ralph, knowing that he had always loved her, being like an elder brother. So she'd confided her dreams to him, telling him how much she longed to escape from Surface Paradise—and now she'd given him another kick!—for that morning he'd confessed that he still loved her and was still tempted by her.

Slowly Anne put on her white knee-length dress with the red hibiscus flowers and strapped on her sandals, then returned to the parlor—only to find Michael fast asleep on the sofa.

"You *do* make yourself at home!" Anne exclaimed.

Startled, Michael sat up, smiling at her and patting the cushion beside him, bidding her to sit down.

"No!" Anne replied, sitting on the wicker armchair beside the round table.

"What happened in Cairns?" Michael asked, again hunching over.

"Really, it was silly," Anne confessed.

"So, it's over?"

"Yes, Tom's accepted it."

"Here I thought I'd lost you. Come over and sit beside me?" Michael again urged, patting the cushion.

"You get your way too easily!"

"What did ya say to Tom Delaney?"

"I told him I love you!"

"Did you?" Michael asked, blushing.

"Yes, I did! Now tell me, why did you sleep with Gloria last night?" Anne asked, jumping up and stepping to the screen door, looking blankly into the hot sand dune before the bungalow.

"There's nothing between us," Michael insisted, standing and coming behind her.

"Why don't you tell me the truth?" Anne asked, turning to face him.

"If you loved me, you wouldn't call me a liar!" Michael retorted, suddenly feeling weak.

"Yesterday in the bus station at Gympie I asked myself if I was doing the right thing in coming back."

Michael was breathing shallowly, feeling that his whole future—their whole future together—was about to go up in smoke.

"Yes, I told myself at Gympie that you were different," Anne again said reflectively.

"Anne!" Michael cried, wheeling about and collapsing on the sofa, pressing his eyes into the sofa cushion.

"It was late when I arrived last night, but this morning I got up early and went down to the beach to speak with you," Anne said with quiet determination. "Ralph was painting his sailboat. Right away I knew that something was wrong with him, for I could see it in his face. I went to the kitchen, and Mrs. Proctor told me straight off that you'd spent the night with Gloria."

Anne's voice was brittle, strained, for she clearly found it difficult to maintain her composure, but then she was determined to face the truth and wanted him to face it too.

Standing up, Michael looked into her eyes. "Anne, I'm really sorry about what happened. It was entirely my fault."

"You seem to have some sense of remorse—but is that all you've got to say for yourself?"

"What do you want me to say?" Michael pleaded.

"I expect it's just different with blokes? Sex is just a game, isn't it?"

"Believe me, I'm sorry!"

"When you offered to help Mummy and me, you seemed so innocent. But obviously, you'd something else in mind!"

"I meant what I said," Michael protested. "I don't know what else to say, but you mean everything to me."

"Then you don't love Gloria?"

"I never loved Gloria!"

"Do you expect me to believe that leopards don't change their spots?"

"I don't know anything about leopards!"

"Don't you, really?" Anne asked in a mocking tone. "When you've enjoyed a lot of women, isn't that rather predictable?"

"I felt wretched when you left. I'd no idea of getting involved with Gloria!"

"Perhaps she seduced you? Do you expect me to take you back, as if nothing had happened?"

"I don't know what to say," Michael pleaded.

"Don't you see that I've some self-respect too?"

"Do you want me to flagellate myself or write a confession letter to the newspaper?" Michael asked, at his wits' end.

"Do drop your tone of habitual cynicism!" Anne pleaded, close to tears.

"Okay, I'll be sweet and nice!" Michael exclaimed, jumping to his feet and pacing back and forth.

"Despite what happened, I still love you," Anne confessed.

Michael stopped and, placing his hands on her shoulders, looked deeply into her eyes. "Anne, I can't live without you. I'd walk across the dead heart of Australia to be with you. I love you and wish to marry you."

"Will you promise to take me away from Surface Paradise, so that I'll never hear the name of Gloria Murchison again?"

"Is that what you want, to get away from Surface Paradise?"

"I don't wish to live here anymore, nor do I ever wish to return," Anne insisted.

"Oh?" Michael said, surprised.

They sat on the sofa, and he put his arms about her, kissing her. Somehow he'd always known she'd be there, even before he knew she existed. Her prominent kneecaps, the angularity of her limbs, the soft brightness that shone in her eyes burned like acid in his brain, like an affliction of memory that was beyond time and space, a subtle poison hidden in the heart of a beautiful flower that only the last flicker of his consciousness would obliterate.

"Michael, if you wish, you can come and stay here and sleep on the sofa," Anne told him, tracing his lips with the tip of her finger as she smiled into his eyes. "You see, I'm not going to take any more chances. I can just see the baffled look of rage on the Old Bat's face when she learns that we're going to get married! And as for Gloria, she'll have to regard the whole episode as a painful learning experience, something she must get through in order to become wiser!"

"Anne, please don't make me feel any more guilty than I do!" Michael pleaded. "I keep askin' myself what I would have done if you'd rejected me."

"From now on, dear boy, you goin' to be on your best behavior," Anne assured him, leaning over to kiss his lips.

Just then there was a sharp knock on the screen door. Michael jumped up and looked at the silhouetted figures in the bright daylight.

"I forgot to tell you that I went down the beach this morning to invite you to come waterskiing on the Nerang River with Robin and Peter," Anne said as she greeted them with a smiling face. "Come in an 'ave a cuppa!"

"'Ow yer goin', mate?" Peter Lutchford greeted Michael as he stepped into the parlor.

"Hi!" Robin Bowles greeted him as well.

Not having anything better to do for the moment, Michael greeted them, annoyed at their intrusion, but wishing to go along with Anne. He was thinking that the breed of young people Down Under looked blonder and healthier than anyone should be, as if the entire generation had been bred in a laboratory by some mad scientist who, by a monstrous oversight or the proverbial absentmindedness of a man of science, had left out the brains.

Peter drove them in his Land Rover over the desiccated landscape to the Cockatoo Bar, where on the verandah they drank a cold tinnie before walking down the gangway to the dock, where the motorboat rose and fell on its short tether, slapped by the river. After climbing aboard, Peter sat in the driver's seat and turning over the engine while Michael, one foot on the dock, the other on the boat, helped the girls to board and then managed to untie the lines and jump aboard without falling in. Then he sat amidship beside Anne.

"'Ave ya got yer bathers on?" Anne turned to ask Michael.

"No, I didn't know we were goin' waterskiin'," Michael said.

"Anne, ya'd better check 'im ta make sure," Peter suggested, a grin on his face.

"You're a bunny!" Anne exclaimed, laughing.

"Then he'll just 'ave ta waterski starko, so you girls will 'ave ta promise ta look forward," Peter said.

"No man is going to remove his clothes in my presence!" Robin protested.

"Little Miss Wowser 'ere, ain't ya?" Peter chastised his girlfriend. "Mike, ya kin borra me swimsuit."

With a dubious expression, Robin turned to Anne for moral support.

"Don't worry, Robin," Anne assured her. "Michael's not goin' ta take his pants off if I've anything ta say 'bout it."

On the bank of the Nerang River, great trees stood in unbroken succession, their adventitious roots reaching down into the river, making weird contortions. The waves lapped into the hollow spaces between the roots, as if the trees were drinking up the river. Great vines hung down from the treetops, with festoons of white, starlike flowers duplicated in the dark surface of the river.

"Well, who wants to 'ave a burl?" Peter asked, easing off on the pedal and turning to Anne and Michael.

"I've never waterskied," Michael confessed.

Peter shrugged, then Anne suggested that Robin and Peter waterski while she drove. Michael stayed where he was while Anne climbed into the driver's seat. Peter and Robin came out of the water effortlessly and glided over the river's dark surface. After a mile or two, when the river narrowed, they dropped off, and Anne turned about to pick them up.

"Now it's yer turn, mate," Peter addressed Michael as he pulled himself into the boat.

"Don't the girls object to seeing a naked man?" Michael protested, grinning. "Besides, I've no wish to commit suicide!"

"Not ta worry, mate. Ya'll be wearin' me swimsuit," Peter replied. "Eyes front, girls!"

Peter pulled off his swimsuit and threw it into Michael's lap. Standing up, Michael pulled off his pants and shorts, then tried to step into the swimsuit, despite the movement of the boat.

"Peter always acts like a larrikin when he's with you—you shouldn't encourage him!" Robin chastised Anne.

"Why do you get brassed off!" Anne flared, a look of challenge in her bright eyes.

"Come off it. All you surfie girls are the same," Robin cried angrily.

"Stuff it!" Anne cried.

"Will ya two stop slangin' each other!" Peter ordered as he pulled on his khaki shorts before turning to Michael. "Doan' they sound like a pair of cats?"

"Best keep outta a cat fight. Oops!" Michael exclaimed, falling headfirst into the river.

Anne turned about to see Michael clutching the side of the boat, one hand on the boat, the other on his swimsuit.

"Anne, gotcher eyeful?" Peter quipped, grinning.

"I'm all set," Michael reported to Peter, having pulled his swimsuit up his long legs.

Peter handed Michael his waterskis, then jumped into the river beside him, holding Robin's skis.

"I'm goin' ta teach ya 'ow ta waterski," Peter began to explain as Michael treaded water beside him. "Doan' start yet, Robin. First, Michael, I doan' wancha strainin'. Just crouch down in the water an' keep yer skis straight in front of ya, unnerstahn'? When Robin starts up, let the water push 'ard 'gainst yer skis till ya feel that yer comin' up. Ya'll get the 'ang of it soon enough."

The motorboat moved slowly, then the rope zinged taut while Michael pushed hard against the skis. He came up out of the river, but just when he thought he'd succeeded, his waterskis crossed and he took a header.

"Fer crissake, Mike, doancha listen ta whot I'm sayin'?" Peter asked angrily as he dropped back into the river.

"Pete, shut yer gob!" Anne flared, jumping into the river and swimming to where Peter had gathered up the waterskis. Taking off her rubber bathing cap, Anne let her dark, flocculent, tightly curled hair glisten in the sunlight.

"Pete thinks I'm a drongo," Michael confessed to Anne.

"We'll show 'im!" Anne replied, pinching his behind, her dark eyes gleaming at him.

Anne put on Peter's waterskis, and soon they managed to get out of the river together, riding on the dark, shining surface as if it were an eel's back. On the banks, the trees moved past as if they'd been painted on a revolving cylinder. Peter shouted to them when he feared they were too close to the bank, for they might hit a submerged root. Moving to the middle of the river, they felt the hot sun on their shoulders between the treetops. After a mile or so, Peter signaled them to drop off, and the water hit them with a splash. They treaded water, holding their skis, while Peter circled around to pick them up.

* * *

Back at the Cockatoo Bar for lunch, they found a table on the verandah under the shade of an umbrella.

"Mike, not bad fer starters," Peter conceded as they sat down.

"Don't you like Australian food?" Robin asked Michael, fixing her blue eyes on him across the table. "Or have you traveled in Europe so much that you prefer French cuisine?"

"Food's never been a big deal with me," Michael said.

"Dere orta be a lore dat if any Frog cook arrives Down Under, he's shot at port of entry, no questions asked," Peter said.

"Michael's very fond of Pom cookin', especially Mrs. Murchison's roast beef and Yorkshire puddin'," Anne said.

"Aussies've got the best tucker in the world, ain't dat so, Mike?" Peter challenged them.

"Ya'll get no argument from me," Michael conceded, turning to Anne. "What's that couple over there havin'?"

"Barramundi," Anne said.

"They must be English," Michael surmised. "I heard them talkin' when they came in."

"Naw, dare from Melbun', I 'eard 'em myself," Peter insisted.

"Michael wants to stay on indefinitely in Oz an' become a beachcomber," Anne said, smiling slyly.

"Beats workin' any day," Peter said.

"Shouldn't we order? The waitress has been hoverin'," Robin reminded them.

"How 'bout the barramundi?" Michael suggested.

"I'm not that financial at the moment, mate, so we'll 'ave the fish-n-chips," Peter said.

"Doan' worry, Pete, I've gotta pay you back for your waterskiin' lesson."

"Thanks, mate, but ya doan' owe me anything."

"Let's go Dutch?" Anne suggested, touching Michael's leg with her bare foot beneath the table.

"No, I insist," he protested, signaling to the waitress and ordering barramundi for them all.

"Better come wi' me ta the loo, so we can swap our togs," Peter reminded Michael when the waitress had left. "Besides, I gotta shake the 'and of the unemployed."

Michael followed Peter to the men's restroom, where recently he'd been locked in a stall.

"I wan' ya take good care of Anne, mate, or ya'll be 'earin' from me," Peter warned Michael as he pulled off Michael's khaki shorts and handed them to him in exchange for his swimsuit. "She's a ripper, mate!"

"Ya doan' have ta worry 'bout that, Pete," Michael replied.

"Yer gaga 'bout 'er, ain't ya?" Peter asked when they left the men's room.

Late that afternoon Peter and Robin dropped Anne and Michael off at the Coleraine bungalow in Surface Paradise before heading back to Brisbane, where Robin was a nurse and went on duty in the hospital. Anne expected her mother to have returned from food shopping, but surmised that she'd gone to the air-conditioned flick to get out of the heat. Going straight to her bedroom, Anne changed into her white knee-length dress with the red hibiscus flowers while Michael sat on the bamboo sofa in the parlor, smoking an herbal cigarette. The room was hot and close, and he began to feel sleepy but feared to kip on the sofa, knowing that he might offend Anne.

When she finally came, she sat facing him in the wicker armchair beside the round table.

"Come over here, Anne," Michael pleaded as he patted the cushion beside him.

"Why? What do you have in mind?" Anne asked him suspiciously.

"I thought I might kiss you," Michael said, grinning.

"That's why I'm stayin' here,' Anne replied, crossing her legs.

"What's that little bird called, anyway?" Michael asked, looking at the stuffed bird in the bell jar.

"It's a male golden whistler," Anne said. "The female is really quite dun; one would hardly notice it."

"That shows how different birds are from human beings," Michael suggested, smiling at her inanely.

"Flatterer!" Anne cried.

"Anne, you look a beaut today. You're a vision of loveliness."

"Please don't, Michael!"

"That's how I feel about you." He pulled himself to his feet and swayed with a look of irritation.

"Why did you insist on paying for Robin and Peter's lunch?" Anne asked, sounding her grievance. "Peter makes good money to pay for them, so you needn't have played the big shot."

"He said all he could afford was fish-n-chips," Michael protested, looking offended.

"Then that's what they should have had!"

"Okay, I'm sorry," Michael said, suddenly deflated.

"Are you going to come and sleep here tonight?" Anne asked, her tone softening.

"Sure, if it's that important to you, of course I will," Michael replied, now hurt.

"It *is* important to me. I want you to stay here until we leave Surface Paradise."

"Why do you act as if gettin' away from Surface Paradise is the end of all your problems?" Michael asked, irritated by the tone she'd taken up.

"Michael, I think Gloria is the right girl for you!" Anne cried, springing to her feet and stepping to the screen door, where she looked into the blank hot sunlight. "Gloria's got style! She'll teach you how to spend your money!"

"Why d'ya act as if spendin' money is such a big deal?" Michael asked, breathing quickly, shallowly.

"It's you who make it a big deal!" Anne exclaimed, turning about to face him. "Why don't you see that Gloria's got a proper education and the proper social background? I think you'd be perfect together, happy with your privileged social life!"

"Except I don't love Gloria!" Michael protested. "And money's got nothing to do with it! Either with the way I feel about Gloria or about you."

"Michael, you can't live in a world stuffed with atmosphere," Anne insisted. "You've no idea of the trials and tribulations of ordinary people. I simply wouldn't fit into your life, for you'd soon come to despise me!"

"Why can't I make you understand that I love you?" Michael said, grasping her arms as he looked intently into her eyes. "Why can't you see that I can't live without you?"

"Perhaps you've never really been serious about anything?"

"Anne, when I first came to Oz, I felt miserable and was a whinging bastard. But then I met Ralph, and we became good friends, and I started down the long road that led to you, as if you'd been there all the time. I always expected you'd be waiting for me, if I could find you. But now that I've found you, do you think that I'm going to give you up?"

"You will come here and sleep tonight?" Anne repeated her question.

"I've told you that I will."

They sat on the sofa, and Michael put his arm about Anne's shoulders, squeezing her upper arm.

"Tell me what you plan to do when you leave Surface Paradise?" Anne asked, turning to look into his eyes, for her head was spinning.

"Anne, I'm thinking that we'll spend a couple years in Europe, perhaps at the Sorbonne," Michael said, speaking breathlessly. "I won't get a degree or anything, because I'd find the university atmosphere to be stultifying. We'll be together, educating ourselves by attending lectures and making contacts with students like us."

"Wouldn't I be a hindrance to you?" Anne asked, searching his eyes for an answer.

"No, you wouldn't. Don't you see that we'd share everything we did together?" Michael insisted.

"Michael, that's why I say that you live in a world of your own making. You haven't thought of me at all, what I want, so I can't imagine why you should want a wife."

"But can't you see that we'll share everything that we do together?"

"Yes, until one morning I wake up to find that you've been sleeping with another woman, someone who suited your fancy—at least for the moment," Anne replied, pushing him away as she sprang to her feet.

"Anne, until I met you, you don't know what a disordered creature I was!" Michael exclaimed, also jumping up. "When the other day I saw you for the first time on the beach, I knew that something unimaginable had happened. I knew that before, my life had been tedious and gray, and if I lose you now, the rest of my life will pass like a nightmare, and I'll wake up a gray-haired old man!"

"How can you pretend to have such high ideals, when you seduced Gloria at the first opportunity?" Anne challenged. "For one who's had so much education, obviously you've no moral sense!"

"Intelligence has nothing to do with the moral sense," Michael explained, flustered.

"In your case, obviously it doesn't!"

"I do regret my behavior with Gloria. I'll admit that I was selfish, that I behaved like a beast, but you've forgiven me, remember?"

"So neither of us has a moral sense. Is that what you're saying? I for forgiving you for being as selfish as myself and for longing to get away from Surface Paradise. Michael, do you really feel that we can be happy together? If we married, I should like to have children. Is that hopeless too?"

"Anne, I don't want anything to come between us," Michael pleaded, taking her in his arms. "I know I'm being selfish, thinking only of myself, but I could get a position with the State Department and be sent to Europe, and we could begin to plan for our future, and having children. You see, I'm only sure about one thing: that I want you with me."

"Will you sleep on the sofa tonight?" Anne again asked.

"Yes," Michael confirmed, kissing her lips and feeling the softness of her breasts.

Suddenly they heard the screen door slam at the back of the bungalow.

"Hello, Anne, are you at 'ome?"

"It's Mummy!" Anne explained as they quickly separated.

"Anne, I've got some lovely crayfish at the fish market, if only Mr. Sykes were 'ere—oh, he is here!" Mrs. Coleraine cried upon passing through the beaded curtain, with Michael standing beside Anne, a sheepish expression on his face.

"Mum, did you go to a flick?" Anne asked.

"Yes, with Mrs. Wilcocks, who drove me, you see, for, Mrs. Sykes, I haven't the use of a car," Mrs. Coleraine explained. "After we'd done our shopping, we come back 'ome. The heat's been wearyin', risin' from the road before the windscreen. 'Ave ya both been for a swim?"

"No, Mummy, do you remember I told you that Peter and Robin would be taking us waterskiin'?"

"So ya did!" Mrs. Coleraine said.

"Mummy, you've 'ad yer 'air done!" Anne exclaimed excitedly. "It does look lovely!"

"Yeah, I got it done before I went shoppin'."

"It looks great!" Michael assured Mrs. Coleraine, seeing that her hair was now a bizarre orange instead of gray.

"An' you've bought a new dress!" Anne cried. "Mummy, you do look a different person. Doesn't she, Michael?"

"Anne, please don't extract compliments from him on my behalf!" Mrs. Coleraine urged.

"I say it looks great on you, Mrs. Coleraine," Michael assured her.

"Mummy, you look twenty years younger!" Anne said. "If I don't watch out, Michael will be making up to you, won't you, Michael?" Anne smiled at him sweetly, parting her lips to reveal her small white teeth.

"Well, I was never one to let myself go," Mrs. Coleraine said, patting her hair and showing a simpering smile.

"Mummy, you might teach Michael how to dance!" Anne giddily suggested, finding the idea amusing while Michael was wondering if his future mother-in-law would come to their wedding wearing a white dress with pink candy-stripes.

"Oh, I'm sure he can do better than me, m'dear," Mrs. Coleraine responded as she sat down on the wicker armchair beside the round table, while Anne and Michael sat on the sofa facing her.

"Mummy, Michael's goin' to come an' live with us," Anne explained.

"Where will he sleep?"

"Right here on the sofa."

"I don't know what to say." Mrs. Coleraine half rose to straighten her dress, then sat down again.

"I doan' wanna be any trouble," Michael insisted.

"Michael, when you get to know Mummy better, you'll find that she always gets her way in the end," Anne assured him.

"Will Mr. Sykes be 'avin' tea with us?" Mrs. Coleraine asked her daughter.

"No, he'll be having supper with the Murchisons, but he'll come back here later," Anne said. "I'll leave the porchlight on for 'im."

"I see," Mrs. Coleraine said, slightly perplexed.

"Anne, I'll be back later," Michael repeated, getting up quickly.

"Michael, have you forgotten something?" Anne asked with a coy smile.

"Oops! Sorry!" Michael exclaimed, stooping to kiss her lips quickly.

20

Walking down the beach, Michael dawdled, finding a smooth, sun-bleached stick in the sand, which he picked up, delighting in the smoothness of its touch. After tossing the stick several times into the blue sky of late afternoon, he threw it into an oncoming comber and lost sight of it. He stopped and stared at the combers, which made their way in stately succession to the shore, where they crashed and rushed up, casting white puffballs before them. Nature at least was honest; deviousness lay only in the heart of man. He wished to be forthright and honest, he thought as he walked along, watching the magnificent waves riding in single splendor to the shore.

There was his stick again as a wave had brought it back from the sea. He picked it up, touched it to his lips, and tasted the salt of the sea. He wished only to be in contact with inanimate nature, under the blue depths of the overarching sky, to allay his self-doubt and recrimination. Evil, he assured himself, is man's own doing, for only man whines and insists on finding pleasure in pain. But if he were to return to the same place as a white-haired old man in some unimaginable future, yearning to die, what compensation would he have for not having lived?

A walk that should have taken Michael fifteen minutes took more than an hour, for his thoughts had been sapped by irresolution, which should have been hidden by a mask. But he was not Julien Sorel in Stendhal's *The Red and the Black*, wooing Mathilde de la

Môle, who was Gloria Murchison; just as Anne was Manon, whom he wooed as Chevalier des Grieux in Prévost's *Manon Lescaut.*

Michael entered the house, fearing that no fictional mask would serve him. He was intent on slipping upstairs, packing his suitcase, and leaving the Murchisons like a thief. But at the foot of the stairs, he encountered Mrs. Murchison wearing the same black, floor-length dress with purple bugle beads she'd worn on their first encounter. Her daughter was beside her in a white, knee-length sheath that looked absolutely wonderful on her Junoesque figure, while Ralph was dressed in a schoolboy's blue blazer, looking like a painfully irritated paterfamilias.

"We're just going to have dinner," Mrs. Murchison announced, offering Michael her arm.

"Shouldn't I dress for dinner?" Michael pleaded.

"No need to. Come as you are," Mrs. Murchison urged as she glided into the dining room on Michael's arm, taking her usual seat at the head of the table.

After seating his hostess, Michael sat facing Gloria, while Ralph sat opposite his mother at the far end of the table. Michael quickly stole a glance at Gloria, who looked perfectly impassive.

She's been through hell! Michael thought. *Yet her face is a perfect cameo, the ideal of the classic, feminine beauty. Why isn't she ranting and raving?*

In his mind's eye, Michael saw Gloria standing on a marble floor, with the mute eloquence of Lucrece before the throne of justice, ready to denounce him as a seducer. He saw himself already condemned, seized upon, bound, gagged, and dragged away from the courtroom. He was stripped, strapped to the rack by masked torturers, who were very subtle in the art of prolonging life in a broken body that would give out life after only the most excruciating pain. At that moment Michael thought of "Coo-ee," Mrs. Coleraine's little bungalow, with its gimcrackery furnishings. It seemed so far away.

But how could it be, Michael asked himself, *with Anne's sweet look of longing in her eyes, asking me to sleep there tonight?*

"Do two young diplomatists have no dinnertime conversation?" Mrs. Murchison asked them in her boldest tone when Mrs. Proctor had left the dining room, having served the roast beef. "Or does feminine company place a restraint on your freedom of conversation? Generally speaking, I prefer light conversation at dinner, for in my day no one ever thought it necessary to educate women, so we were condemned to idle chatter."

"Men much prefer idle chatter from women, Mummy," Gloria observed, looking at Michael across the table. "Isn't that so?"

"Women have a different sort of intelligence than men," Michael ventured, his eyes meeting Gloria's.

"Are you referring to women's famous intuition?" Gloria asked him.

"No, I mean intelligence, but a different sort of intelligence," Michael insisted.

"When I first came to Australia, I quickly learned that there was little social intercourse between the sexes," Mrs. Murchison reflected. "Women weren't particularly catered to by the men."

"I've always regarded women as a civilizing influence," Michael insisted, looking from Gloria to her mother.

"Isn't that a moral influence?" Gloria pointedly asked him.

"Yes, of course," Michael replied, blushed.

"I am pleased that you find that women have a moral influence," Mrs. Murchison assured him.

"Actually, the Australian male is a perfect hedonist," Gloria explained in a challenging tone. "He'll worship his mother and sisters, but all other women he regards as fair game, for he certainly has no conversation with them."

"That's 'cause the sheilas aren't interested in what interests a bloke, and vice versa," Ralph interjected.

"But, dear brother, after marriage men are no different," Gloria retorted.

"As fer as I can see, onc't a sheila's married, she talks 'bout nothin' but the kids, shoppin', an' holidays," Ralph countered.

"Michael, don't you think that my brother talks down to women?" Gloria asked.

"Doan' be askin' Mike a question like that, 'cause he'll talk with anyone," Ralph protested. "He'll chat up a sundowner, a no-hoper, or a metho artist, not to mention any assorted dill. When we go ta King's Cross, he'll chat up a prossie."

Michael's face burned scarlet.

"One night this floozy blonde done up ta the nines leans over the bar ta give Mike a look at 'er norks, with 'er lips all puckered up longin' fer a kiss, with Mike explainin' Neet-chee's *Superman*, fer crissake."

Michael shuffled his feet beneath the table, as sweat trickled down his sides.

"What did you do this afternoon?" Gloria pointedly asked.

"In my time, it wasn't proper to ask a young man what he did," Mrs. Murchison rebuked her daughter.

"I walked along the beach and read," Michael explained, blushing again.

"Don't you think that a man and a woman should be able to talk on a wide range of subjects?" Gloria asked him.

"Yes, I think so," Michael agreed, not elaborating.

"What ya jabberin' 'bout, Gloria?" Ralph said. "Fer most blokes life's slavin' away in a borin' job fer the wife an' kiddies, so ya can't blame a bloke fer turnin' ta 'is mates for some fun."

"I hope you don't share my son's view?" Mrs. Murchison asked her guest.

"No, I say that women play a civilizing role," Michael replied.

"Precisely, women bring peace and order," she said. "No man wishes to live in a bear garden, or to be slanged at by his wife for that matter."

"Why don't women direct their energies into a larger sphere?" Gloria asked.

"Because, Gloria, most women are content with a good marriage," Mrs. Murchison contended in a tone of admonishment.

"Mummy, how can you say such a thing when you regret your own marriage, having left the London stage behind for the back of the beyond?"

"All I'm attempting to say, m'dear, is that a woman can do exactly what a man does, but will still find that she prefers a good marriage. Of course, there are always exceptions, but that doesn't bear either way."

"It's these women's mags that make the sheilas discontented with their lot," Ralph observed, with a smile of smug complacency.

"My brother ignores the fact that many of these journalists are men," Gloria informed Michael.

"Any bloke that works fer a wimmin's mag is either a poofter or a Pom, so ya can take yer choice," Ralph insisted. "Ya can see 'em drinkin' in Paddo an' chirpin' like sparrows."

"Michael, have you noticed how insecure the Australian male is regarding his masculinity?" Gloria asked in her challenging tone. "The greatest fear of the Australian male is that someone might think him a homosexual. But don't you think that mateyness is an unconscious form of homosexuality?"

"Hardly, m'dear," Mrs. Murchison replied, taking up the gauntlet. "The Australian male may be unpolished, but he has the innocence and simplicity of nature about him, for he is as calm and serene as the Bush. Money means very little to him, because where he lives it has scant value."

"Mummy, don't you think the nation would be better served if we were governed by women?" an unrepentant Gloria inquired.

"What then would men do, m'dear?" Mrs. Murchison asked. "Certainly, you wouldn't expect them to stay home and change nappies?"

"They could have the babies as well, as far as I'm concerned!" Gloria exclaimed. "But my question was not yours, Mummy, but our guest's."

"If a woman waited to be asked her opinion, she'd be dead!" Mrs. Murchison cried, laughing.

"Really, Mummy!" Gloria exclaimed. "Michael, what do you think a woman should do?"

"She should do exactly what a man does," Michael blurted out.

"That's oreright, just so long as she goes back to bein' a woman when she's finished," Ralph interjected, also laughing.

"How my brother must despise women!" Gloria said.

"All the sheilas do today is tell blokes they're discontented," Ralph retorted.

"They say if you scratch an Aussie, you'll find a sheepshearer," Mrs. Murchison observed, alarmed by the turn of the conversation.

"The trouble is that Oz 'as never been civ'lized," Ralph said with a faraway look in his eyes. "When I was just a little nipper, I went on the Indian Pacific to Perth with Dad, and right in the middle of nowhere, I saw a farm'ouse with a windmill standin' beside it. I can still see the windmill turnin' in the sunlight and water gushin' outta a pipe into the trough. When I nudged my dad, he just looked at me an' said, 'That's a mirage.' When I looked back, I found that it 'ad disappeared before me eyes as fast as it came. Thot's the water that should irrigate Oz, so that people can live here, but there ain't no water."

"I much prefer a house where generations have lived," Mrs. Murchison announced. "A green-tilled land where human happiness is the only concern, for who was meant to inhabit a desert?"

* * *

After dinner Mrs. Murchison proposed her nightly game of whist, but Michael pleaded a headache and retired immediately. He had pulled his suitcase from under his bed and was stuffing it with the contents of the dresser when there was a sharp knocking at the door.

"Doin' a moonlight flit, are ya?" Ralph said, looking brassed.

"Yeah," Michael confessed, not trusting himself to say more as Ralph sat on the straight-backed wooden chair before the window, tilting it back and thrusting out his legs.

"Good thing too, 'cause ya've behaved like a rotter," Ralph charged. "So I won't appeal to your better nature, as Mum did at dinner this evening, 'cause I think yer beyond that. But I've got one question ta ask ya: 'ave ya rooted me sister?"

"Listen, Ralph—" Michael began, looking at his friend.

"Answer me question, yes or no."

"Look, Ralph, I don't have to—"

"Yes or no!" Ralph repeated, pulling himself to his feet.

"No!" Michael exclaimed.

"'Ave ya rooted Anne?"

"Look, Ralph, you're not goin' to play judge and jury!" Michael protested, breathing heavily, although he could understand Ralph's concern.

"Mum believes you've a sense of honor, that ya'll do the right thing, but will ya?"

"You've no right to ask me that question," Michael protested.

Ralph placed his hands on Michael's shoulders and looked closely into his eyes. "Mum says yer a decent bloke, one who will—"

"Ralph, this is really none of your bus'ness."

"Mum says thot ya won't marry Anne, 'cause she wuz our maid. Mum's thot way, ya see, but I doan' see ya changin'. Mum's attitude at dinner shocked me, ya see, 'cause she doan' mind ya bonkin' every sheila in Surface Paradise, 'cause she'll forgive ya, if ya marry 'er daughter 'cause ya've got the lolly."

Michael turned away, making no response.

"Do ya love Anne, then?" Ralph asked.

"Yes, I do," Michael confessed, feeling miserable.

"So there's nothin' fer it?"

"No, nothing."

"Ya took the bait like a gudgeon?"

"Ralph, I can't live without her. I've asked her to marry me."

"So the old monster of egotism 'as been smashed, is thot it?" Ralph asked, enjoying his friend's humiliation.

"Utterly smashed to bits! But I don't wish to lose you as a friend. Your friendship means everything to me."

"Forget it!" Ralph responded, punching Michael lightly on the shoulder. "D'ya wan' me ta drive ya up to Anne's?"

"No, thanks. I'll walk along the beach. But will you please apologize to your mother on my behalf? I couldn't face speaking with her."

"Doan' worry 'bout that!"

"Ralph, this mornin', when I saw you and Anne together, I realized—"

"Whot's that?"

"You still love her, but I'd no idea. It came as a surprise to me."

"'Course it did, ya bloody egoist," Ralph retorted with a forced smile.

"I do really hope that we can still be friends."

"Doan' worry 'bout thot, mate!"

Michael gave Ralph a bear hug.

* * *

When he was alone, he lay on his back on the bed, smoking an herbal cigarette, while breathing rapidly and shallowly. He thought that it was best that Ralph should thank his mother for her hospitality, for sometimes it is necessary to be cruel in order to be kind, especially when words won't suffice. His unspoken thoughts were suddenly interrupted by a knock at the door. Michael sprang to his feet and saw Mrs. Proctor, who said, "Mrs. Murchison would like to speak with you in the living room."

"Tell her I'm leaving"—he abruptly changed course—"that I'll be right down!"

Steeling himself, Michael closed his eyes, then walked down the hall feeling like a sleepwalker, even though his eyes were wide open. Mrs. Murchison was seated on the love seat, with an unstoppered brandy bottle and two glasses on the coffee table before her. She greeted him with a radiant smile, motioning for him to take the seat beside her, which he was reluctant to do. Immediately she poured him a brandy, without asking if he wanted one, then she left the brandy unstoppered.

"I'll come straight to the point," Mrs. Murchison began. "My son has told me that you propose leaving tonight?"

"Yes, I expect that Ralph has also told you that I'll be staying with the Coleraines, for I plan to marry Anne," Michael responded.

"And I told him that I did not believe a word of it!" Mrs. Murchison exclaimed, fixing her dark eyes upon him. "Of course, what you tell me is painful, but I do admire your candor."

"Thank you. I'll be leaving tonight," Michael reaffirmed as he poured himself another brandy.

"Do you know what my son has told me?" Mrs. Murchison asked. "He tells me that I've played a very foolish game, and that I've lost."

"I can't tell you how much I regret what has happened," Michael confessed. "How badly I feel about my behavior, ever since I arrived in Surface Paradise."

"The chickens have come home to roost; isn't that an American expression?" Mrs. Murchison asked, pouring herself a generous glass of brandy.

"I guess so, but I do regret my behavior," Michael again confessed, reaching for another brandy, before Mrs. Murchison enveloped him in her arms, pressing her ample bosom against him, and kissing him on the forehead so that he felt like a little lost boy. When he was released, he saw the tears in her eyes as she began fumbling in her bosom for her handkerchief. Afterward she poured herself another brandy and another for himself.

At first, Mrs. Murchison sipped her brandy in silence. "It is my opinion that young men know no law of heaven or earth," she announced. "They only find it incumbent upon them to sow their wild oats." She continued in this vein for several minutes, while Michael's face turned crimson, for he hadn't spent many years plucking roses on the primrose path of dalliance.

Finally Mrs. Murchison came to the point. "Michael, I have a request to make of you. Will you delay your departure for the fortnight you have promised to stay?"

"It would be unfair of me to stay a moment longer," Michael protested, embarrassed to have been caught looking at his watch, which told him that it was after ten o'clock.

"Unfair to whom?" Mrs. Murchison challenged.

"Er, to Gloria," Michael said.

"Do you really imagine me capable of taking such offense?"

"Mrs. Murchison, I can't stay another night in this house!" Michael insisted.

"I ask that you simply keep your promise that you will stay with us a fortnight. Surely that's not asking too much of your generosity? Certainly it's too late to go up there, for the Coleraines will already have gone to bed. The first thing in the morning, you must go up there and explain the reason for your delay. Or you might ring them?"

"They don't have a phone. Besides, I'd rather explain it myself," Michael protested, beginning to rise.

"Not even if I ask you from the bottom of my heart?" She grasped his right arm and made him sit down again.

"Mrs. Murchison, evidently you believe that I'll change my mind about Anne, but that won't happen. Actually, my conscience is bad enough in this matter, without you trying to impose some sort of penance on me."

"But surely if your love is so strong, it can withstand an insignificant delay?" Mrs. Murchison urged.

"It can, I'm sure, but—"

"Then why don't you put it to the test?"

"Why?"

"Are you afraid you will achieve a new perspective?"

"No, of course not!"

"Why then?"

"All right. I'll stay, if it means so much to you."

"Thank you. That is all I ask," Mrs. Murchison said, rising to embrace him and plant a kiss on his cheek before sweeping majestically from the room.

Alone, Michael hunched over, pressing the heels of his hands into his eye sockets.

Mrs. Murchison is right, Michael finally assured himself. *It's too late to go to Anne's tonight. But what if Mrs. Murchison has set me a trap? She wouldn't do that. Besides, I can afford to be generous. As Ralph says, "Mother's really thinking of her social position." It would be humiliating if I were to leave so abruptly.*

In this mood of complacent self-assurance, Michael went upstairs to retire for the night. But no sooner had he opened his bedroom door than he saw Ralph lying on his stomach on the bed, reading *The History of the Australian Seventh Division.*

"Mum lent ya this book, did she?" Ralph asked, getting up and tossing the volume onto the dresser.

"Yeah."

"So what did Mum tell ya ta do?" Ralph demanded, confronting his friend.

"Why should I tell you, when you'll immediately go downstairs and tell your mother?" Michael asked, annoyed.

"Tell *'er,* ya mean, whot she already knows?"

"Well, your mother has asked me to delay my departure for two weeks. I thought I owed her that much at least."

"Fer crissake, d'ya know whot ya've done?" Ralph asked angrily.

"I shall explain the circumstances to Anne in the morning," Michael announced.

"Mike, Mum thinks ya've capitulated. Ya've given Mum time ta maneuver. Look, Mike, me mum's views of the male are doubtless not original, but she's given you enough rope ta hang yerself."

"Don't dissuade me from doing what I think best!"

"Mike, not an hour ago, ya stood 'ere an' tol' me that ya couldn't live without Anne. Doancha see that Mum will let ya 'ave yer little fling with Anne, an' when it's over an' ya've seen reason, ya'll—"

Michael exploded. "Ralph, I don't need your mother to tell me what my duty is!"

"Righto, Mike. Let me leave ya ta yer sweet dreams!" Ralph stepped to the door, opened it, and turned around. "I'll be takin' the *Sea Lark* out fer 'er first spin first thing in the mornin'. Wanna come?"

"Sure, okay," Michael replied, hardly able to think what he was saying.

Michael switched off the light, pulled off his clothes, and lay naked on the bed. The air was still and hot, sapping any moral resolve, even though the sun had set long since. Turning onto his back, Michael saw the light burning on the front porch of the Coleraines' bungalow, where Anne was waiting.

21

The following morning, Michael awoke from a sharp rapping on the door and the peremptory summons "It's gone eight, mate! Are ya comin' sailin' wi' me in the *Sea Lark*?"

"Com'on in," Michael groaned, springing to his feet and pulling up his underpants, followed by his khaki shorts.

"Why doancha' eat some 'nanas. Yer all skin an' bones," Ralph commented as Michael pulled his T-shirt over his head. "Ya musta fergot thot yer comin' sailin' wi' me?"

"Ralph, I believe that I should have taken your advice an' cleared out last night," Michael confessed. "In the light of mornin', I can see that I've made a damned fool of myself. I shoulda gone straight up the beach an' explained to Anne why I didn't go las' night."

"Ya can speak ta 'er downstairs."

"Whaddya mean?"

"Anne came back this mornin' ta werk fer Mum. Right now she's in the kitchen helpin' Mrs. Proctor ta make one of 'er lovely lamb an' kidney pies. Just wait till ya taste it; it'll make yer mouth water."

"Anne came back to work for your mother?" Michael asked, dumbfounded.

"Yeah, Mum tol' 'er she could start right away."

"Why should she come back here?"

"'Cause she needs the lolly, mate, an' jobs is as scarce as hen's teeth 'ereabouts."

"Look, Ralph, I must speak with Anne," Michael said, sitting down on the bed and strapping on his sandals.

"'Ave it yer way. Ya usually do, mate!" Ralph yelled before leaving the room and slamming the door behind him.

Michael flew downstairs to the kitchen, where Mrs. Proctor had Anne standing before the sink, wearing a maid's uniform and with her elbows in a sink full of water, soaping pots and pans. The sunlight came streaming through the window, refracting into shards of light through Gloria's terrarium on the windowsill.

"Anne, I've got to speak with you alone!" Michael exclaimed, standing at the zinc-topped table where Mrs. Proctor was rolling dough. "Mrs. Proctor, will you excuse us for a moment?"

"Well, I never!" Mrs. Proctor cried, not budging.

"Whatever you've got to tell me can be said in front of Mrs. Proctor," Anne announced, finally turning to him.

"I want to explain why I didn't come to your bungalow last night, and I do have an explanation," Michael said.

"Yer very good at explanation, ain't ya?"

"The fact that I didn't come last night has nothing to do with my love for you."

"Didn't I say you'd have an explanation?" Anne asked sarcastically.

"Anne, lemme explain!" Michael said, stung by her retort, grabbing her arm.

"Lemme go! Yer hurtin' me!" Anne cried, her eyes aflame.

"Anne, I'm not goin' to lose you," Michael said, releasing her. "I want you to come away with me."

"An' 'ave Mrs. Murchison gi'me the sack?" Anne asked.

"Bugger Mrs. Murchison!"

"Well, I never!" Mrs. Proctor sniffed, leaving the kitchen.

"Anne, I'm going to take you away from Surface Paradise. Don't listen to what anyone tells you."

"I've 'eard too many of yer excuses," Anne replied, though she was relenting somewhat.

"Anne, I beg of you, give me this last chance," Michael pleaded, reaching to touch her right arm as if she were a vision that might vanish before his eyes. Anne smiled, knowing that her greatest battle had been won as she untied her apron and went to speak with Mrs. Murchison. "No!" Michael cried, suspecting what she was about to say.

"Can't I tell Mrs. Proctor that I'll start work on Monday, if things don't turn out?" Anne pleaded.

"No, we're leavin' Surface Paradise for good!"

"What about yer kit?"

"Ralph will bring it later."

"Then we'd better bring somethin' to eat," Anne said, like a good housewife. She grabbed the dillybag and dropped into it half a loaf of homemade bread, two boiled eggs, a pot of crab paste, a jar of raspberry jam, two bananas, and a thermos filled with orange juice.

They left the house by the kitchen door and were halfway up the sand dune when they saw Ralph sailing the *Sea Lark* close to the shore, with the sail looking almost lifeless.

"If we head up the beach, he'll see us. Let's have the picnic at the Spit!" Michael quickly suggested.

Soon they were walking along the red-earth road, beneath trees held in a suffocating embrace by overarching vines. Michael thought of being there with Gloria, collecting plants for her new terrarium. Sweat trickled from his scalp down his forehead, stinging his eyes. The sickly sweet fragrance of flowers suffused the air, giving it the smell of a funeral parlor.

Reaching the Spit, they left behind the dense luxuriance of the jungle for the sun-bleached glare of the sand and dry spinifex grass. The sand ribbing spoke of a place that had not been disturbed, perhaps never, as if they were the last two people on earth, content with its quiet proximity, without the need of speech. They'd passed through an alien country where tigers crouched in hidden coverts, but they hadn't gone back, for there was no other conceivable future without each other. Now no longer alone, Anne could still remember the emptiness of the midnight bus at Gympie, after breaking up with Tom, when he found out that she and Michael were in binary orbit, revolving about each other, he the bright star and she almost unperceived.

They sat in a hollow on the summit of the Spit between clumps of spinifex grass. Below lay the blue lagoon bound by the coral reef, save for the white channel that marked the entrance, beyond which lay the deep blue of the South Pacific Ocean.

Michael pulled off his T-shirt and searched the dillybag, explaining, “I haven’t had any breakfast.”

“Lemme,” Anne suggested, opening the jar of crab paste and spreading it on two slices of bread, which she pressed together.

“Thanks!” Michael took a big bite, then a swig of orange juice.

Anne watched as his throat muscles moved up and down, thinking that when they’d gone waterskiing she’d seen his naked body in the Nerang River, feeling the hollow, dulcet pain of first love, not knowing what it meant and asking herself if she still loved Tom Delaney and was merely duping herself.

“I want us to get married as soon as possible, tomorrow or the day after, at the latest,” Michael said to her as he looked at her face, appearing like the ghost of the moon in the bright sunlight.

Is Anne disowning me, turning from me because of my lies? Michael kissed away the fears that he saw in her eyes as she ran her fingers up his spine, feeling the bumps.

“The last time I ate a crab sandwich was with my dad in the Savoy Grill in London,” he told her with a bright smile.

“I always thought you were a snob!” she exclaimed, laughing.

“Really?”

“Michael, where will we live when we’re married?”

“Anywhere we please.”

“Will you be working all the time?”

“Only if I need to, but I shall chuck my job at the American Legation and find some honest yakka. Whaddya think?”

"I think you'd make a dinkum Aussie, but don't you live on Long Island?"

"Yeah, an' sooner or later we'll settle there, and I'll throw a big bash, like my dad used to do, inviting all my friends to show them the new bright star in the firmament. Then we'll be very smug and complacent, have kids, and go to Europe each summer, because, Anne, I love you!"

"I love you too, Michael," she replied, as if she saw their happiness spelled out in white letters on the blue sky.

"Let's go for a swim?" Michael asked, standing up when they'd finished eating.

"I don't have my bathing suit."

"What does that matter?"

"I should feel naked without my clothes—more naked than evidently you do!" Anne exclaimed, laughing.

"Don't believe it!" Michael said and pulled off his khaki shorts and underpants together, which he rolled into a bundle with his T-shirt.

"Michael, you have beautiful narrow hips."

"I'll be waiting in the water for you."

Slithering down the Spit, Michael dashed across the narrow strip of sand and plunged into the water, which had no cooling effect. He swam out to the middle of the lagoon, then dove to the sandy, sunlit bottom. Swimming back to shore, he saw that Anne had left her clothes on the beach and gotten in after him. She emerged from the water looking like Venus coming from the sea, saying, "How beautiful I am!" Her hands instinctively rose to cover her breasts, then, undecided, they rose to her dark hair, revealing the sensuous lines of her body.

"Will you take me to live in your kingdom by the sea?" Michael asked her.

"You'll have to sprout gills first," she said with a bewitching smile.

"That's easy!" he shouted, plunging beneath the surface again, his legs sticking up like poles.

Coming up to her, he took her in his arms, feeling the softness of her breasts against his chest, which felt cooler than her body. They swam out, skirting the coral reef that protected the Spit from cyclonic storms. When they swam back to the beach and emerged from the sea, they were like Adam and Eve, the first couple. Anne retrieved her clothes as they climbed the Spit. They spread their clothes out and lay on their stomachs beside them in the hollow declivity of sand to dry in the sunshine.

"You are Venus come from the sea," Michael whispered into her ear, so that when she turned, he fell into her bright, sparkling eyes.

"Michael," Anne said, as if she'd never spoken his name before.

Beyond the admonishment of words, Michael knelt beside her, taking her in his arms, kissing her shoulders, her throat, as she murmured, feeling the awakening of a deep responsive chord, for she already knew that they were on the crest of a wave and that she could do no wrong by withholding herself.

Yet the first time was different from what she'd expected, sensing his eagerness, and she found herself eager to answer his expectations. She had an inexplicable hollow need in her for him, for she felt as light as a feather, certain of the truth in the weight of his body. Afterward, she placed her head on his chest and listened to his heart beat.

"What more have we got to eat?" Michael asked, looking into her bright eyes and seeing the satisfaction of their love.

"Two hardboiled eggs, a few slices of bread, two bananas, and a pot of raspberry jam," Anne said.

Sitting up, Michael fished a hardboiled egg from the dillybag and began carefully to peel the eggshell.

"Do we go divvies now on everything?" Anne asked him.

"Gotcher!" Michael responded, a mischievous grin on his face as he popped the whole peeled egg into his mouth.

Anne pounced on him, pushing him into the sand, as amid a fit of coughing and laughter, he disgorged the entire egg.

"Now I'll have to wash it in the sea," he protested.

Michael began sliding down the Spit, but halfway down he fell against the sand and crawled back upward, calling, "Anne! Ralph's offshore in the *Sea Lark*!"

"He's seen you. He just entered the lagoon!" Anne said as they quickly put on their clothes.

"I know yer both up there!" they presently heard Ralph's voice calling from below, where he'd beached the *Sea Lark*. "Do I 'ave ta surprise ya two lovebirds?"

"We might just as well show ourselves," Michael told Anne, standing up and waving to Ralph, who was climbing the Spit.

Anne looked red-faced with embarrassment, so Ralph put his arm about her, squeezing her waist in reassurance of her love for him. "Whaddya see in this long streak of pelican shit?" Ralph asked her. "I say he's a first-class bastard! Tell me if I'm wrong."

"Yer wrong with knobs on it!" Anne retorted, laughing.

"I see I wuz wrong, 'cause ya've got love written all over yer faces," Ralph conceded. "'Ave ya got any tucker in the dillybag?"

"Just some bread 'n raspberry jam," Anne said.

"I've got some 'ot tea in the boat, if ya wan' some?" Ralph offered. "Maybe ya'd both like ta come for a spin?"

"I'd love to, Ralph—wouldn't you?" Anne appealed to Michael, who'd remained quiet, seeing that Anne gravitated to Ralph, just as if they were still lovers.

"I do b'lieve the poor sod's jealous," Ralph reminded Anne. "You doan' know 'ow much I envy you, an' 'ow pleased I am fer ya!"

"Yer a sweetie, Ralph," Anne cooed.

"Thanks, Ralph," Michael conceded, looking constrained.

"This poor sod doan' know 'ow ta be 'appy!" Ralph exclaimed, laughing at his friend's expression.

"Give 'im time ta get used to it," Anne urged, looking up into Michael's face.

After they'd eaten a slice of raspberry jam, they went down to the *Sea Lark* and drank a cup of hot tea before they pushed the sailboat off the beach and climbed aboard. Michael sat amidship beside Anne while Ralph manned the tiller. Propelled by a slight breeze, the *Sea Lark* glided across the lagoon and breached the coral jaws of the channel cut into the reef before they felt the seaswell. Offshore the breeze picked up at a good clip, and the sail was taut. Michael turned to see the Spit rising from the sea, looking as if it had no connection with the earth, for the shoreline had dissolved into a gray line.

"Ralph's an excellent sailor," Anne assured Michael, after their skin was wet from the spray.

"I'll 'ave ya both back on land in an 'our!" Ralph confidently predicted as the wind rose.

Michael began to feel queasy, and he was overcome by a great lethargy. He lay on the slats, his head in Anne's lap, hearing a clock ticking, and when he opened his eyes, he was lying in bed at home. His father entered the room, sitting on the edge of the bed, saying, "Son, you're lucky to be alive."

* * *

Michael remembered what had happened; he'd been out in the rubber life raft and lost the oars, watching them being flipped by the wind over the sea. He'd realized that the raft had gotten away from him, so he had tried to swim ashore, seeing the slate roof of his father's house between the willow trees that lined the shore. Alternating between a crawl and a backstroke, he'd finally felt the seaweed that lined the rocks, where he'd held onto the ladder at the dock, feeling exhausted.

"Bail! Bail!" Michael heard Ralph call, as a blinding flash lit the sky, the thunder reverberating in their chests. A great commotion filled the air, as if the wind were coming from all directions of the compass. Michael sat up and saw that the horizon was gone, with the rain bouncing on the sea like a musket shot.

Anne got two coffee tins from the forward compartment and began bailing furiously, but they made little progress although, miraculously, the wind had abated, and a calm light shone above the sea.

"It's over!" Michael shouted, seeing the Spit looming above them with pallid insubstantiality.

"In just a moment, it'll hit us again," Ralph direly announced, a strange calm in his voice.

"Ralph, we'll get through the reef by then," Anne confidently predicted, smiling at Michael to give him courage.

Almost as she spoke, a banshee howling caught the *Sea Lark*, divesting her of her sail, which flew off like a seabird. Anne screamed as Michael was thrown overboard and found himself underwater. When he came to the surface, the *Sea Lark* was perched precariously atop the coral reef. Swimming painfully to the side of the sailboat, Michael hoisted himself up, but the sailboat was empty. The ocean was pouring through the breach in the coral reef, as if into some fantastic chasm.

"Anne! Anne!" Michael cried, but already the pain was sifting through his limbs, sweetly solicitous, rising to blot out consciousness.

"Anne! Anne!" Michael called again, suddenly seeing a white plume blooming in the lagoon beside him. He gathered her in his arms in her white maid's dress, which was attached to her by one arm; he disentangled it before swimming to the beach. Her eyes were closed, and her face was washed by the sea. The sandy bottom abraded his arms as he picked her up on unsteady feet; he stumbled onto the beach and lay her down naked on the sand. Kneeling beside her, he ran his fingers along the dark line of hair at her right temple, where there was a faint gash. She opened her bright eyes and uttered his name, but she seemed lost in an ineffable dream that he could not share.

"Wait, we must go home now," Michael told her.

"I must go now to where no mortal can come," she told him.

Michael lay down by her side on their marriage bed, for she told him what he already knew: she would be his bride forever.

EPILOGUE

Michael opened his eyes to see a flat white ceiling. The air smelled sickly sweet with flowers, although there were no flowers in the room, but only the sunlight streaming through the window. Propping himself up on his elbows, he felt a peculiar sensation, as if his stomach had been scored by a razor. Pulling himself to a seated position, he moved his feet to the floor. He unbuttoned his pajama top and saw that his torso was encased in plaster. Pressing his hands down against the bed, he stood on unsteady feet, a dark cloud pressing down upon him, despite the brilliance of the sun as he reached the window. Below was a garden with a brick wall, with palms and flower beds and crisscrossing macadam paths that led to a central pond. The surrounding buildings denoted a city, for he could hear the unseen traffic.

"Mr. Sykes! What do you think you're doing?"

Michael turned to see a stout woman in a nurse's uniform, her cap perched on gray hair, bearing down on him like a locomotive. She seized him between her arms and dragging him back to the bed. Feeling dizzy, Michael feared that he'd pass out, but she made him lie down and be tucked up tightly, so that the sheet seemed to restrain him.

"Where am I?"

"In 'ospital."

"How long have I been here?"

"A week. The very idea!"

"A week? Get me outta here!"

"With broken ribs an' a gash in yer side, you'd 'ardly any blood in ya when they found ya," the nurse admonished him. "Yer lucky ta be alive!"

"I must leave!"

"The doctor will say when ya can, but there's a young lady been comin' ta see ya," the nurse said. "If ya wish ta see 'er, I'll send 'er in."

"Anne!" Michael exclaimed, sitting up.

Gloria looked smart in a tan linen suit, despite the heat. Michael could see the pain in her eyes.

"Gloria, where's Anne?"

"I've come to tell you about that," Gloria began, her voice faltering. "After the accident, you were both brought here, and at first the doctors thought she might live, but I'm afraid it wasn't to be. It was two days before they found my brother's body."

"Anne's dead?" Michael asked, unbelieving.

Michael saw the tears welling in Gloria's eyes as she turned and looked blankly out the window. Slowly, feeling the pain, he turned onto his stomach as if they were strangers, pressing his face into the pillow. Gloria turned back and placed her hand between his shoulder blades, thinking to console him, for he shook with bitter sobs.

She did not stay long, knowing that she could not allay his bitterness, for at that moment she felt that she would never see him again. But the following afternoon, she reappeared, not speaking of the accident. He listened absently, having little to say, for he'd lost the will to live, or so Gloria felt when she spoke to the doctor, who told her that it might take longer than anticipated for him to get back on his feet.

"Tom Delaney came down from Cairns for Anne's funeral," Gloria explained to him the following day. "I hope you'll understand. When I told him that you were in hospital, he bore no grudge, saying all that he wanted was Anne's happiness. Robin and Peter were at both funerals, and Anne's mother had us back to Coo-ee for a funeral lunch. Oh, and Tom Delaney said that if ever you wanted an honest day's yakka, he'll get you drovin' sheep."

"Is Tom sheepshearing now?" Michael asked.

"Yes, he gave me his address in Barcaldine," Gloria explained, fishing in her handbag. "I have it somewhere. Imagine your undertaking such a life? Here it is, Bulloo Downs."

Michael held the slip of paper, looking at it wistfully.

The next day, Gloria paid her last visit before returning to her job in Sydney. "You won't leave Australia without saying good-bye?" she asked him.

"Of course not," Michael replied.

"What will you do when you get back to the States?" Gloria asked him.

"Haven't given it a thought," Michael confessed, looking into her dark-brown eyes.

"I suppose you'll write to me sometimes and tell me what you're doing?"

"Sure, I don't want to lose sight of you," he replied casually.

When Michael was discharged from hospital in Brisbane, he visited Mrs. Coleraine at Surface Paradise, then flew to Sydney, where he submitted his resignation at the American Legation. It took only a few days for him to pack up his belongings, mostly books accumulated during the two years he'd spent in Australia, and have them sent home by steamship. On his last day, he had dinner with Gloria at a Greek restaurant on Macquarie Street.

"I'm goin' home by sea," Michael told her. "I've booked on the *Oronsay*, which sails at noon tomorrow."

"Shall I see you off?" Gloria asked.

"You'd better not."

"You don't like good-byes?"

"I hate 'em!"

The next day Gloria appeared before the ocean liner sailed.

"I expected you'd come," Michael told her.

"I've brought you Tolstoy's *War and Peace* to read on the voyage," Gloria explained, handing him the two-volume Penguin.

"Thanks, I'll have lots of time to read," Michael said. "Good-bye then."

"Good-bye then," Gloria repeated. "I predict that one day you'll make a lot of money and never think again of Oz!"

"I won't forget," Michael protested, putting his arms about her and kissing her briefly on the lips.

* * *

Gloria had brought colorful streamers, which she gave to Michael to throw from the boat deck, and she caught one amid the press of passengers. The ocean liner moved backward from the terminal beside the Circular Quay near the Harbor Bridge, so that the streamers broke one by one, fluttering into the water like twisted snakes.

"Coo-ee!" Gloria called to him from the terminal.

"Coo-ee!" Michael called back from the boat deck, cupping his mouth, although Gloria's face was indistinguishable in the throng. The crenellated Conservatory of Music drifted past as the *Oronsay* turned to the Heads to cross the Tasman Sea in the bright sunlight to New Zealand.

* * *

During the following year, Mrs. Murchison died, and Gloria sold the house and land at Surface Paradise, which was turned into building lots. With a part of the proceeds she bought a bungalow at Killara on the Pacific Highway just north of Sydney. She wrote to Michael that since he'd left Australia, she'd been leading a quiet suburban life with no interesting relationships and deriving little satisfaction from her position with the magazine.

"I think that middle age is not far off!" Gloria had concluded.

Michael went to work with Sykes, Price & Co., but after the death of Justin Price, his son-in-law, Jud, took charge. Life for

Michael had fallen into a familiar pattern. He had an apartment near Washington Square, but spent the weekends on the North Shore of Long Island, where his housekeeper, Mrs. Tucker, seemed perfectly able to manage without him. Michael began taking Jud's wife, Jaine, to dinner and the theater, while Jud was busy in the office, so that Michael soon found himself in the ludicrous position of being encouraged by his business partner to dance attendance upon his wife, even protesting that his wife was much happier since his partner had reentered the firm.

After a Sunday afternoon tennis match, Michal and Jaine were seated on the circular bench under the beech copper near the tennis court when Jaine confessed, "Of course I'm not happy with Jud!" She opened her china-blue eyes and shook her blonde hair. "You know that Jud and I were married so that I would spite you? Or don't you know?"

Michael had not foreseen that it would come to this. Like Gloria Murchison, he felt that he'd become middle-aged.

"After all, how far can you go to prove a point, or has that never occurred to you?" Jaine protested.

Remaining silent, Michael feared that any response would be taken as limp.

"Of course I really should have left Jud ages ago."

"Really?"

"Yes, really, if you weren't such a coward, totally lacking in moral courage!"

"Look, Jaine, I'm not going to stay in the firm," Michael confessed. "I've decided to go to Europe to study."

"How can you!" Jaine exclaimed. "Jud's overworked as it is! That's what's behind his compulsive drinking. You've no idea what it's like to have to live with him!"

* * *

That fall Michael took a flat in the Latin Quarter in Paris and attended lectures in philosophy at the Sorbonne, taking a crash course in French at Berlitz. A few days before Christmas, he received a redirected Christmas card from Gloria containing a letter; he had not heard from her in some time.

Killara, NSW
December 12, 195—

Dear Michael,

Still at Killara, as you can see, enjoying my half acre of bush and boulders, with a lovely verandah—and a sight of the Pacific Highway!

Recently, I was sent to Brisbane for the magazine and decided on the spur of the moment to visit Surface Paradise. Mrs. Coleraine is now Mrs. Kelleher, the proud owner of the Hibiscus Guest House; to wit, Mummy's old house. The alterations in the house are quite hideous, with frightful bungalows seen everywhere. How Mummy would have been shocked! You will remember how Mummy hated Surface Paradise, keeping the larrikins and sheilas at bay behind her fence? But now they have midnight beach parties and listen to South Sea Island Joe playing the piano at the Surface Paradise Hotel. Or they buy hot mushrooms from Beverly Stafford, the dishonest beachcomber. Or go to keg parties at the Cockatoo Bar on the Nerang River.

But I dimly do recall that that boozer has a place in your chequered history!

Enough of this foolishness! Let me just conclude by saying that I'm often thinking fond thoughts of you this Christmas season.

With much affection,
Gloria

Michael thought that such gush didn't sound much like Gloria, but he was feeling older and feeling world-weary, and was as undernourished as ever.

After taking the long flight to Sydney, with two nights spent en route in Asia, Michael found himself sitting on Gloria's verandah when she drove up in her Morris Mini Minor.

"Michael!" Gloria exclaimed, getting out of the car.

"Gloria, would you like to go to Luna Park?" he asked with a wry smile as he put his arms about her and kissed her lips, holding her for a long moment.

"Have you come all the way from Europe to take me to Luna Park?" Gloria asked as they parted, but she was still holding his right hand.

"How 'bout dinner tonight, then?" Michael suggested.

"We'll have to, as I haven't got anything in—unless you fancy a frozen meat pie from the fridge?"

"What about that Greek restaurant on Macquarie Street in Sydney?"

"Do you wish to go there?"

"Not particularly."

"Then let's eat here."

"While Gloria took the meat pies from the freezer locker, Michael slipped his arms about her and asked, "Gloria, will you marry me?"

"I was expecting to hear you ask me that!" Gloria replied, turning to him.

"Does that mean yes?"

"Yes," Gloria confirmed, and they kissed again. "This does call for a celebration, even though I don't happen to have a bottle of champagne."

"What about this?" Michael asked, producing a bottle of red Australian wine.

They lingered for a long time over dinner, then sat before the fireplace, catching up on their lives.

"It's too late for me to put you out for the night," Gloria finally suggested. "If you don't mind, you might sleep on the sofa."

Surprised, he said nothing.

"I don't want to start *that* way, not until we're married," she insisted. "I hope you're not offended?"

"No, I promise I'll be a very good boy, no monkey business," he said, grinning.

"Did you have a favorite sports or film star when you were a boy?"

"Yeah, the Yankee Clipper."

"Isn't that an airplane?"

"No, it happens to be a baseball star."

"Isn't baseball like our cricket?"

"No, but it's too late for me to get into a big argument."

The following week Gloria and Michael were married in a registry office in Sydney. They flew to Brisbane, planning a fortnight's honeymoon on Moreton Island, which they cut short because Michael insisted that they visit Surface Paradise and see Mrs. Kelleher before leaving Australia.

Mrs. Kelleher greeted them at the front door, looking more energetic than Michael remembered, with her red face and the reek of cheap perfume.

"Ev're room 'as got its own fridge," Mrs. Kelleher said as he put his arms about her, kissing her cheek.

"Gloria, don't ya look the lady, but you always did!" Mrs. Kelleher greeted her before they kissed.

"So lovely to see you, Mrs. Kelleher," Gloria responded loudly enough to overcome the TV in the guests' sitting room, formerly her mother's living room. Immediately Gloria saw her mother's theatrical memorabilia adorning one wall, as it had done for a long time.

"It adds a nice touch, don't ya think?" Mrs. Kelleher said. "Now, what's become of my Bill?"

"'Ere, Madge!" a male voice boomed as a heavyset man with short, iron-gray hair and wearing a stained T-shirt and soiled khaki shorts flip-flopped into the sitting room.

"Bill, meet Gloria an' Mike," Mrs. Kelleher said.

"'Ow ya goin', mate!" Bill greeted Michael, grasping his hand with a bone-crushing mitt. "Willya 'ave a coldie—an' whot 'bout the missus?" Bill kissed Gloria.

"Doan' be daft, Bill!" Mrs. Kelleher interjected. "Gloria an' I'll be 'avin' a cuppa."

"Sounds lovely!" Gloria exclaimed. "Mrs. Kelleher, do let me help you?"

"An' ya'll be 'avin' a coldie wi' me?" Bill asked Michael again, when the women departed.

"Okay, thanks."

"Sure ya doan' wan' somethin' 'arder?"

"No, thank you," Michael insisted as Bill produced two coldies from the fridge, conveniently located in a corner of the sitting room. Sitting outside on rocking chairs, they looked over the sand dune where chalets were perched for holidaymakers. Rock-and-roll music filled the air from portable radios. On the beach were brightly colored umbrellas with groups of young people, for the larrikins of Surface Paradise had triumphed over Mrs. Murchison with a vengeance, but she was dead and in her grave.

"Do you still work?" Michael asked Bill above the din.

"No, I'm retired now. The on'y work I do is 'bout 'ere."

"Where *did* you work?"

"I wuz a butcher in the abattoirs in Brissie," Bill said.

For lunch Mrs. Kelleher served Michael's favorite crayfish salad.

"Are Peter Lutchford and Robin Bowles still living here?" Michael asked Mrs. Kelleher during the meal.

"Oh, they're mister and missus now," she said. "He's gone ta work fer BHP at Whyalla, where Robin's a nurse. I got their Christmas card yesterday an' can give ya their address."

"An' Tom Delaney?" Michael asked next.

"He's still at Cairns, but was at their wedding an' is the same as ever."

After lunch Michael took Mrs. Kelleher aside, asking, "Is Anne buried nearby?"

"Just up the coast road in the new cemetery," Mrs. Kelleher said.

"May I go there?" Michael asked.

"Are you quite sure that would be a good thing?" Gloria asked, appearing from nowhere to grasp her husband's arm.

"Yes, I'm sure," Michael insisted, looking into Gloria's eyes.

That afternoon Mrs. Kelleher drove them to the new cemetery on the coast road in her Holden, parking just inside the front gate, where they walked on crushed seashells to the back of the cemetery. The white limbs of a gum tree were blooming with pink corellas, which, startled, departed en masse into the blue sky, leaving the limbs looking as fragile as human bones.

That night, unable to sleep, Michael slipped from the bed and went downstairs like a sleepwalker, out into the moonlight. Going down to the shore, he walked north to the spot where Anne's bungalow had once stood, its roof no higher than the surrounding sand dunes. Climbing the dune, he saw the pale moonlight shining on the bungalow and stumbled toward the front porch. A dog barked, and a light was switched on, so Michael turned, lurching toward the sea, calling, "Anne! Anne!" He was unreconciled to his loss, and nothing could alleviate the pain he felt.

Gloria found herself alone, and a fear gripped her heart. Wearing only her dressing gown, she went out into the moonlight, walking north along the shore, half wondering, half fearing what she would find.

"Michael! Michael!" Gloria called out.

She found him lying on the hard wet sand by the shore, having been rejected by the sea, for the sea had told him, "Not yet … not yet," and he knew he would have to go on living without her.

That morning Michael and Gloria left Surface Paradise and never returned again, nor wished to.

* * *

In the firm founded by his father, Michael has become a respected bond trader, to which his partner, Judson Jones, will attest.

Michael and Gloria have a boy and a girl, and people say that Gloria speaks with a British accent, which amuses her and would please her mother, so she does not disabuse them. Each summer the couple spends a month traveling on the Continent, so that their children will have the cultural advantages of Europe.

In December Michael receives a Christmas card from Mrs. Kelleher, along with a chatty letter; he never speaks of Anne, for she has become a part of his lost youth, even if at moments when he is staring into the white mist above the sea he knows that she is there, ever present as the earth, the sea, and the sky, part of the everyday brightness of the world.

AUSTRALIAN WORDS

Abo: Aborigine
apples: Okay, all right
arsed out: Departed
back of the beyond: Remote, inaccessible
back teeth: Fed up
beaut legs: A beautiful woman's legs
billabong: A waterhole
billy: A tin can for boiling water to make tea
bloke: A man
bonkers: Crazy
bonkin': Having sexual intercourse
boozed: Drunk
brassed off: Bad-tempered, annoyed, disillusioned
bullocky: Violent language
bunk: Run away, take flight
burl: To attempt, to try
bush: The country, the Outback
bushed: Tired, exhausted
bushwacked: The same
bushwalking: Walking in the bush
chook: A chicken
coo-ee!: A prolonged call to attract attention
chump, the head, do his chump: To get angry
cobber: Mate, friend

codswallop: Rubbish, nonsense
coves: Men
cow-cockeying: Small dairy farming
da: Father
dicey: Risky, unreliable
dill: A fool, incompetent
dillybag: A small bag for food and personal belongings
dingbat: An eccentric or peculiar person
dinkum: True, honest, genuine
dollybird: An attractive young woman
dreamtime: The time when the earth received its present form and seasons (Aborigine)
drongo: A slow-witted, stupid person
dunny: Toilet
financial: Needing money
flick: A movie
flit, moonlight flit: To leave quickly at night
fluttered: To confuse, to make nervous
footy match: A football game
gaga: Besotted
gob: Mouth
gotcher!: "I've got you!"—indicating comprehension or agreement
Great Republic: The United States
gudgeon: A small fish, but here, one who is easily duped or cheated
hols: Holidays
humpy: A shelter or bush hut
invite: Invitation
kip: To sleep
kit: Clothing, personal articles
Kiwiland: New Zealand
knobs on it: With enthusiasm
larrikins: Louts, hoodlums
Limey: An Englishman
lolly: Money

lubra: Aboriginal woman
mate: Friend, buddy
mateyness: Good-natured friendship
meat axe, mad as a meat axe: To be angry
meat pies: A pie made with pastry
metho artist: Addicted to methylated spirits
mozzies: Mosquitoes
nappies: Diapers
narky: A complainer, a nagger
natter: Chatter, gossip
navvy: Laborer
Never-Never: Sparsely inhabited country
nig-nog: A Negro or dark-skinned person
ninny: A fool or simpleton
no-hoper: An incompetent, a social misfit
norks: Female breasts
orange squash: A soft drink
Outback: Sparsely populated, back country
Oz: Australia
Paddo: Paddington, a suburb of Sydney
peckish: Having an appetite
pelican shit (that is, a long streak of pelican shit): To express annoyance or frustration
pervin' me: To look at a woman with sexual desire or longing
piss, on the piss: To drink beer
plonk: Cheap wine
Pom: An Englishman
poofter: A homosexual
prossie: A prostitute
quadruple-lord: An alcoholic drink
quid: A pound (money)
righto!: An expression indicating agreement
ripper girl: Someone exciting and admirable
root: To have sexual intercourse

roustabout: A handyman on a sheep station
Second Basho: The Second World War
sheila: A girl or a woman
Sinny: Sydney
sleeping like a top: To sleep well
slippy: Nimble, quick
soup, the soup: A wave
sod: Poor fool
squiffy: Tipsy
stringy-bark: A eucalyptus
Strine: Australian English
stroppy: Rebellious (from *obstreperous*)
Surface Paradise: The novel; a place; Michael goes gaga over the surface of Anne's body, for she is the eternal feminine
sundowner: A swagman
swag: A bundle of personal belongings carried on the shoulder
swagman: A man who travels about the country living on the earnings from occasional jobs
Tassie: Tasmania
tinnie: A can of beer
to-do: To fight
too right!: An expression of agreement
tucker: Food
two-up: A game played with pennies
unemployed (that is, to shake the hand of the unemployed): To urinate, to have no sex
walkabout: An Aboriginal period of wandering, seeking to replenish in the bush
water butt: A container to collect water
Wet: The rainy season
whinging: Complaining
wowser (that is, Little Miss Wowser): A prude
yakka: Work
yobbo: A loutish or surly youth

Printed in the United States
By Bookmasters